PRAISE FOR MARIE FERRARELLA— AUTHOR OF SEVENTY-FIVE SILHOUETTE NOVELS!

"Marie Ferrarella is a charming storyteller who will steal your heart away."

—*Romantic Times* magazine

The Baby Came C.O.D. (SR #1264):
"Marie Ferrarella pens another winner…. As usual, Ms. Ferrarella finds just the right balance of love, laughter, charm and passion."

—*Romantic Times* magazine

"This is a hilarious, slapstick read…. It will leave you in stitches while wanting more."

—*Rendezvous*

Do You Take This Child? (SR#1145): "The strong romantic flavor…will win the hearts of romance fans everywhere." —*Romantic Times* magazine

Father in the Making (SR#1078): "Lively, heartwarming characters make this poignant romance…a read to cherish."

—*Romantic Times* magazine

Wanted: Husband, Will Train (SE#1132): "This is an irresistible, sparkling and sometimes funny story. Absolutely delightful." —*Rendezvous*

"Taking a classic plot and adding her own humor and passion, Ms. Ferrarella gifts readers with a grand romance." —*Romantic Times* magazine

Dear Reader,

Silhouette welcomes popular author Judy Christenberry to the Romance line with a touching story that will enchant readers in every age group. In *The Nine-Month Bride,* a wealthy rancher who wants an heir and a prim librarian who wants a baby marry for convenience, but imminent parenthood makes them rethink their vows....

Next, Moyra Tarling delivers the emotionally riveting BUNDLES OF JOY tale of a mother-to-be who discovers that her child's father doesn't remember his own name—let alone the night they'd created their *Wedding Day Baby.* Karen Rose Smith's miniseries DO YOU TAKE THIS STRANGER? continues with *Love, Honor and a Pregnant Bride,* in which a jaded cowboy learns an unexpected lesson in love from an expectant beauty.

Part of our MEN! promotion, *Cowboy Dad* by Robin Nicholas features a deliciously handsome, duty-minded father aiming to win the heart of a woman who's sworn off cowboys. Award-winning Marie Ferrarella launches her latest miniseries, LIKE MOTHER, LIKE DAUGHTER, with *One Plus One Makes Marriage.* Though the math sounds easy, the road to "I do" takes some emotional twists and turns for this feisty heroine and the embittered man she loves. And Romance proudly introduces Patricia Seeley, one of Silhouette's WOMEN TO WATCH. A ransom note—for a cat!—sets the stage where *The Millionaire Meets His Match.*

Hope you enjoy this month's offerings!

Mary-Theresa Hussey
Senior Editor, Silhouette Romance

Please address questions and book requests to:
Silhouette Reader Service
U.S.: 3010 Walden Ave., P.O. Box 1325, Buffalo, NY 14269
Canadian: P.O. Box 609, Fort Erie, Ont. L2A 5X3

Marie Ferrarella

ONE PLUS ONE
MAKES MARRIAGE

Silhouette
ROMANCE™
Published by Silhouette Books
America's Publisher of Contemporary Romance

In the memory of Miss Anne J. Nocton,
who took a shy, awkward fifth grader and made her see
her own potential.
Thank you.

 SILHOUETTE BOOKS

ISBN 0-373-19328-9

ONE PLUS ONE MAKES MARRIAGE

MARIE FERRARELLA

lives in Southern California. She describes herself as the tired mother of two overenergetic children and the contented wife of one wonderful man. The RITA Award-winning author is thrilled to be following her dream of writing full-time.

Dear Reader,

In *One Plus One Makes Marriage,* I have the opportunity to share with you a little of one of my passions—old movies. The heroine was raised in the movie business and thus has a clear view of reality while still believing in the magic of life—and love. It's a lesson she finally manages to pass on to the hero, but not easily. Therein, hopefully, lies the entertainment.

This book is rather special to me. It marks my seventy-fifth book with Silhouette. I remember the exact moment I sold my very first book to Silhouette. I was in the shower. My agent called to tell me the good news, and it was like getting a reprieve from heaven. I was seven months' pregnant with our second child, and my husband had been laid off for thirteen months from a very depressed aerospace industry. The wolf was not at our door yet, but he was circling the area. Thanks to Silhouette and you, he never arrived. I've been writing for Silhouette for fifteen years now, and I still feel as if I'm in the honeymoon stage of a wonderful marriage. So far, I've had seventy-five "children"—how's *that* for a world record?—and a world full of neighbors to come and enjoy them with me.

All my love,

Marie

Chapter One

"I've never seen such a wonderful collection of photographs. And all autographed, too."

Staring at the uniquely decorated wall for a moment, the small, matronly woman's gray eyes became as round as a child's, lighting up her face and adding color to the almost-translucent, sagging skin. Wrinkles and stiffness, the outward heavy signs of her advancing age, magically faded. Like twin beacons breaking through a thick fog, her eyes scanned the back wall of the shop again, picking out familiar, well-loved faces of movie stars, many long gone except for the miracle of celluloid. She sighed in what sounded to Melanie like ecstasy.

The reaction pleased Melanie. Melanie McCloud had hammered in every single nail herself that supported the 126 photographs, painstakingly recreating Aunt Elaine's old parlor.

Her shop, Dreams of Yesterday, now had the atmosphere of a cozy room, where someone could seek refuge from a frantic world for an afternoon—the way she had so often in Aunt Elaine's parlor, she remembered fondly. It was there that the photographs had originally hung. Most of them were personalized with a salutation from a movie star, and some had short notes, all directed to her late aunt.

Melanie smiled to herself as she silently watched the woman next to her. The woman's excitement grew in direct proportion to her recognition of the various celebrities. It was her first time in the shop, and she didn't know where to look first, afraid of missing something in her scattered, shotgunlike approach to viewing the photographs.

"Oh, look, there's Rita Hayworth." She sighed again, beaming. Without being fully conscious of it, she patted her own strawberry-tinted hair as she commented, "Such a beauty." Turning her head a fraction of an inch, the woman spied another star. "And Tyrone Power. My mother was just crazy about him. Oh, and Errol Flynn." Standing on her toes, she looked closer at the inscription, then blushed over the risqué message written in a bold hand across the actor's bare chest.

Melanie bit her tongue to keep from laughing. That particular photograph, one of her aunt's treasures, was not for sale, but she knew her aunt would have gotten a kick out of having people see it. As a matter of fact, she would have insisted they see it. She was proud of the fact that the handsome actor had come on to her in print.

The elderly woman paused and turned toward Melanie, astonishment mingled with the joy of discovery. That was half the fun of owning a place like this—seeing the way people reacted to items that she had, for the most part, taken for granted while she was growing up.

Scarlet nails fanned out as the woman touched Melanie's arm in instant, intimate camaraderie. "Tell me, my dear, where did you get all these wonderful things, and who is Elaine?''

It was evident by the look on the woman's face that she thought Elaine was in an enviable position, to have known so many great stars.

''Elaine was Elaine Santiago, my great-aunt.'' There was pride in her smile. There was little that Melanie loved more than reminiscing about her aunt.

''Was?'' A tinge of disappointment entered the woman's voice.

Melanie nodded. ''She died a little over two years ago. But she left me her collection of memorabilia.'' Melanie gestured around the shop. ''About half of all this was hers.''

The rest Melanie had gone out of her way to acquire for this little shop in Bedford, California, like the large shipment that had arrived just this morning, thanks to a successful afternoon at a Hollywood memorabilia auction. She couldn't wait until she closed up tonight, so that she and Joyce, her partner, could go through everything. Not just to see if it was all there, but just to enjoy it.

The woman looked at the wall again, still overwhelmed by the wealth of photographs hanging on it. ''She was a big movie fan?''

That was putting it mildly, Melanie thought. Aunt Elaine had crammed her head full of colorful stories and a myriad of trivia by the time she was old enough to read. Aunt Elaine was a walking font of information and she never forgot anything.

''The biggest. She worked at MGM in the wardrobe department for years, then went over to Paramount Studios, where she went on to become a makeup artist.'' For someone like Aunt Elaine, the job had been a dream come true. And everywhere Aunt Elaine went she made entire platoons of friends. She believed it was her mission to leave everyone's life a little brighter for knowing her. In Melanie's opinion, she succeeded beyond her wildest dreams.

"In her time she knew them all. Everybody loved Aunt Elaine. That was what they all called her, Aunt Elaine." And that was what she'd tried to be, everyone's aunt. The thing about Elaine Santiago was that she truly cared about people. And everyone knew it. "She always seemed to know when someone had a problem, and she was always willing to lend a sympathetic ear. No one could keep anything from her. She was exceptionally easy to talk to."

Melanie grinned, remembering one of her aunt's favorite stories. "Burt Lancaster once said to her that she could probably get a stone to talk. She had that way about her."

The greatest compliment Melanie had ever received was when someone had compared her to her aunt. Her mother had put a slightly different spin on it, saying that she could coax words out of a mime, but it was one and the same, Melanie mused. She and Aunt Elaine loved people, all manner of people.

A hint of envy entered the gray eyes. "She must have been a remarkable woman."

She'd get no argument from Melanie. "She was, in every sense of the word." Melanie still missed her fiercely. She knew a part of her always would.

"Melanie, you want to come here a second?" Joyce Freeman's raised voice broke apart the easy tempo of the conversation. When Melanie turned in her direction, Joyce gestured with a touch of urgency that was underscored by the frown on her small mouth. "I think some-one here wants to talk to you."

There was a nervous note in Joyce's voice. So what else was new? Joyce wasn't happy unless she was wor-rying about something. Melanie gave the woman at her side an encouraging smile.

"You'll excuse me?" she murmured, beginning to back away. "Feel free to browse as long as you like. I'll be back to answer any questions in a minute. Maybe two," she amended as she glanced again in Joyce's di-rection and saw the depth of her best friend's frown. Even from across the shop, it looked pronounced.

It undoubtedly had something to so with the tall man who was standing beside her. Melanie lengthened her stride, hurrying over while still giving the impression of taking her time. She could feel the man's scrutiny as she drew closer. Curiosity began to sprout.

"Something the matter?" She directed the question to Joyce, who looked positively ready to leap out of her skin.

There was confusion in Joyce's dark brown eyes. She didn't really care for change in general and absolutely abhorred the unknown. The unknown was standing at her side in the form of a very tall, very somber-looking man with charcoal gray eyes and the darkest shock of black hair Melanie had ever seen.

Hair, she thought, that looked like velvet. The kind of velvet found on the inside of a really expensive jewelry box used to hold valuable, well-loved rings. For a sec-ond, looking at him, Melanie couldn't help wondering if his hair felt as soft as it appeared.

Without thinking, she almost reached out to touch it before she caught herself. Would that have made the man's frown retreat? Or merely deepen?

Melanie's eyes shifted back to her friend's face. There was no relief evident at her approach. If anything, her expression of concern had intensified. Now what? Melanie tried to shrug off the tiny kernel of concern that was beginning to root within her. It was all probably nothing. Just Joy's way.

They complemented each other that way, Melanie thought. Joy, in direct contradiction to her nickname, worried about inventories and bills, about things that might happen and things that didn't happen, while Melanie, with what Joy dubbed her terminal optimism, went along assuming the best would somehow manage to push its way through any dark obstacles that stood in its path.

Melanie absolutely refused to spend her time worrying. She firmly believed that if something was going to go wrong, it would happen without her obsessing about it, and if it didn't go wrong, then worrying that it might would have been a waste of energy and time. She made Joy crazy, especially since most of the time she was right.

Joyce licked her lips. She slanted a nervous look at the man. "I'm afraid he thinks something is the matter."

Melanie smiled at the stranger with the clipboard in his hand. A wish list perhaps? It wouldn't be the first time someone came into the store clutching one. Maybe Joyce was upset because they didn't have any of the items on it. She wouldn't put it past Joy.

"Can I help you with anything?" Melanie asked engagingly.

There was a dimple appearing and disappearing in her cheek, as if unable to decide whether to remain, as she smiled at him. Lance Reed watched for a moment in fascination despite himself. A snappy answer to her

MARIE FERRARELLA   13

question, which several of the guys at the firehouse would have easily uttered, played across his mind, never making it to his lips. And with good reason. It was largely unrepeatable.

He took quick measure of the petite blonde who'd blown in his way like a sweet, cool breeze on a warm spring day. Unlike the woman he'd been talking to, she didn't appear to have a care in the world. She also didn't seem to be aware of the errors she was guilty of committing. Or, if she was, she didn't care. He guessed that the latter seemed more likely.

That innocent look on her face was probably purely calculated for effect, he decided. Beneath the wide smile and wider eyes lay a devious mind. Lance Reed was well acquainted with the type. Hell, he'd been engaged to the type.

The blonde opened her mouth. The dimple set up housekeeping, calling forth a twin in her other cheek. She was going to flirt with him, he realized. Well, she could flirt until she was completely out of breath, wiles and charm. It wasn't going to do her any good. She wasn't going to talk her way out of a citation. Which would be for her own good. Or at least the public's.

Certainly liked to stretch things out, didn't he? Melanie thought. She raised a questioning eyebrow in Joyce's direction, but Joy looked positively spooked. What was going on here?

"I'm sorry, maybe you didn't hear me. I said, 'Could I help you with anything?'" Melanie repeated.

"I heard you," the deep voice rumbled. But before answering her question, Lance checked off several items on his clipboard.

He'd only taken on the job of fire inspector a little less than two months ago, helping out until someone

permanent could be hired to take the place of John Kelly,
who had just retired. He wore two hats these days, one
as a fire inspector and his regular one, that of an arson
investigator. It wasn't easy, juggling the two, but there
wasn't much else to fill his hours the rest of the time
since Lauren was permanently out of his life.

Thoughts of Lauren, of the way she had just turned
and walked away when he had needed her most, dragged
sharp, rusted nails through wounds he'd thought he'd
finally managed to cordon off so that they could heal.

Showed how much he knew, Lance thought ruefully,
disgusted with himself. His mood was not the best as he
focused on the blonde standing before him and tapped
the clipboard. "It's not me you're going to need to help,
Ms. McCloud."

"Melanie," she corrected, trying to put him at ease
with her smile. Being addressed by her surname put
much too formal an edge on things. Tutored by her free-
spirited mother and equally uninhibited great-aunt, for-
mality was something that had never taken root in Melanie's life.

From the way the stranger looked, it had obviously
not only rooted, but flourished in his. He made her think
of a soldier, standing just at the line of battle a moment
before going into the fray.

An extremely good-looking soldier, she noted. If Aunt
Elaine were still around, she'd have been drooling, Melanie thought fondly. Aunt Elaine had always had an eye
for good-looking men. It never waned, not even when
she was in the hospital. Melanie liked remembering her
that way. Aunt Elaine had flirted with a young intern
moments before permanently closing her eyes. She died
with a smile on her lips.

"And who is it that I'd need to help?" Melanie asked,

wondering if she was going to have to coax every word out of this man's mouth.

Her voice was low and melodious, Lance thought. He wondered if that was a put-on. Probably. The next moment she'd be batting her lashes at him. It seemed in keeping with the old-fashioned decor in the shop. When he'd first walked in, he'd had to take a minute to adjust. Not his eyes, but his orientation. Crossing the threshold had been like walking in through a time warp. Outside, in the bright California sun, it was the nineties; in here, it was like being thrown headfirst into the early fifties. Or maybe even earlier than that.

Retro wasn't his thing. It obviously seemed to be hers. There was an old record player in the corner, its spindle laden with a stack of what looked like long-playing albums, the type that had been made when vinyl records were the only kind available. The music floated along the perimeter of his mind, vaguely familiar, even though he thought that wasn't possible.

It was the theme from an old movie, he realized, before he shut the sound out. Something he'd probably heard as a kid.

He wasn't here to play "Name that Tune," Lance reminded himself, he was here to do his job and move on.

"You're part owner of this store," Lance nodded at the shop, "aren't you?"

Just what was this about? Melanie exchanged glances with Joyce, whose lips seemed to have lost the ability to form words.

"Yes."

Though she had owned all of the inventory before she'd decided to open up the shop, Melanie had insisted that Joyce become equal partners with her. It seemed only fair, seeing how many hours they both put in. Besides, it felt right, and Melanie always went with what felt right. Like her friendship with Joy. Living on the same street, they'd been friends since before kindergarten. Actually, only Joyce had gone to kindergarten. Melanie had remained home, to learn at her mother's elbow. Her mother's and Aunt Elaine's, as well as several tutors her mother had brought in.

Melanie was firmly convinced that she'd learned far more from the two women, about life and surviving as well as the usual subjects, than she ever would have in a school where knowledge was contained within four walls and within the pages of books. Her classroom had been the world in general and the movie set in particular. Or rather, behind the movie set, where drama and magic, make believe and truth played equal parts.

"Then these citations belong to you." Removing the sheet from the clipboard, Lance handed it to her. It listed five direct violations of the fire code, and he knew he could have given her more.

Melanie glanced down at the sheet, then back up at the man who had given it to her. She shared a little of Joy's confusion. "You're a fire inspector?"

"Yes, and your shop, Ms. McCloud, is a fire waiting to happen." Disapproval was etched on his chiseled, rigid features. Though some might find a place like this charming, Lance didn't care for small, cluttered places. He liked wide-open spaces. The less people allowed junk to pile up, the less fuel there was for a fire and the less likely it would be for a fire to break out.

With the tip of his pen, Lance pointed toward the four huge boxes that had been delivered this morning. "Do you even realize that you're blocking an exit with that stack of crates? If there was a fire, someone could be hurt because of your carelessness.''

The delivery man who'd brought in the shipment had looked and sounded as if he was coming down with a cold. Taking pity on him, Melanie had sent him away after he'd dropped off the crates right inside the rear of the shop rather than in the storeroom. Customers had arrived, and she just hadn't gotten around to putting the crates into the storeroom.

Melanie eyed the inspector. The complaint seemed minor enough to her. Rules, except for the very basic ones, were meant to be a little flexible. Surely he could cut her a little slack. John Kelly always had. A kind, jovial man in his late fifties, the other fire inspector and she had hit it off the first time he'd walked into her shop. But then, he was an old movie buff, and they'd found a great deal to talk about even before he'd discovered that she'd practically grown up in movie studios.

''Yes, but—''

If she thought she could talk her way out of this, she was in for a surprise. He wasn't a pushover, the way the recently retired inspector had been. Lance had seen the power of fire, watched it as it licked its way through a lifetime's worth of possessions in less than ten minutes. There were no second chances with fire, no time to bargain or talk your way out of the havoc it brought.

Lance shook his head. ''There is no 'but,' Ms. McCloud. Something is either a fire hazard or it isn't. And that,'' he tapped the pile of crates nearest him for emphasis, ''is a fire hazard. If you had a fire,'' he repeated pointedly, ''and the people in your store tried to get out this way, they could be burned to death.'' Glancing around, he judged that the whole place could go up like a tinderbox.

There was no reason to feel a fire would start here, Melanie thought. No one was allowed to smoke in the shop, and she'd just had the wiring checked, although, she noticed, according to the stone-faced inspector's findings, the light switch in the storeroom was suspect.

"They could use the front door," she suggested, trying her best to remain cheerful.

He knew better. Firsthand. "What if that way was inaccessible?"

He made Melanie think of someone who'd had what he believed to be an epiphany and now knew the "right" way when everyone else around him was still groping around in the dark. Rather than become irritated, she felt rather sorry for him. Inflexibility was a cross.

"Then I'd push the crates aside," she responded easily to his question, still hoping to coax him into a smile.

Lance's eyes narrowed until they were two gleaming points of a very sharp sword. "Fire isn't a joke, Ms. McCloud."

"I never said it was." Melanie glanced at his name written in small, precise letters on his badge and cocked her head. "Do you have a hearing problem, Lance?"

Annoyance deepened the tiny furrow between his brows. He didn't care for the way she made the leap from being a stranger to someone who was on a first-name basis with him. "No, why?"

"Well, you didn't hear me when I asked you to call me Melanie, and you obviously thought you heard me say that fire was a joke when I didn't." She raised and lowered one slim shoulder. "I just thought that perhaps you had trouble hearing things."

Melanie glanced over her shoulder. The woman she'd left standing before the wall of photographs was still there. Reading her body language, Melanie knew she was ready to make her purchase. Momentarily ignoring Lance, Melanie placed her hand on Joy's arm.

"I think that lady's about to buy something, Joy." She nodded toward the customer. "Why don't you go over there and wait on her?"

There was nothing Joyce wanted to do more than to get as far away from the man with the dark, accusing eyes as possible. He made her feel guilty even when she hadn't done anything. But she didn't want to leave Melanie to cope with him by herself, either. Though she was younger than Melanie by several months, Joy felt very protective of her. Walking away right now would be tantamount to tossing a babe to the wolves.

Chewing her lower lip, Joy weighed obligation against self-preservation. "I don't know, Mel—"

Melanie placed both hands on Joyce's shoulders and turned her around toward the woman. "Never keep a customer waiting, remember?" She gave Joyce a little push in the right direction. "It's okay," Melanie assured her with confidence. "Everything's going to be just fine."

Melanie turned toward Lance as Joyce made her escape. "Isn't it?"

He shrugged noncommittally. "After you pay your fine, that's up to you."

Stubborn, that was the word for him, she thought. Still, she was nothing if not optimistic. Melanie approached the offending stack. "Why don't you just let me move these crates, and then you can erase the check marks on that line? I was planning to put them in the storeroom, anyway, after I close up tonight."

Yeah, right, Lance thought. He'd heard that excuse before.

There was a dolly standing against the wall. Melanie

began to scoot it under the bottom of the stack, but Lance laid a hand on her arm to stop her.

Fool woman was going to get a hernia, or have her head cracked open with a flying crate Lance thought in disgust. Not his problem, he reminded himself, releasing her. His job was to cite fire code violations, not poor judgment.

When she raised eyes the color of crystal spring water in January and looked up at him, it took Lance a moment to remember what he was saying.

He cleared his throat. "That's not how I operate, Ms. McCloud."

Melanie moved the dolly back into place and sighed. He was going to be a tough nut to crack, to use one of Aunt Elaine's favorite sayings. He seemed determined to keep this on a cold, impersonal level. Okay. For now.

Melanie tried her best to be cooperative. "Just how do you operate, Lance?"

When she called him by his first name, she mysteriously seemed to take away some of his leverage. He meant to get it back.

"That's Inspector Reed." An efficient movement of his hand drew her eyes to his badge.

He could almost feel her eyes scanning his name and absorbing only the part she wanted to. The woman clearly had selective vision. You'd think that with eyes like that, he mused, she could see everything. Not only were they the lightest shade of blue he'd ever seen, they were also the most intense.

So intense that they looked capable of seeing straight into a man's mind.

Now there was a stupid thought, Lance upbraided himself. Where the hell had that come from? He wasn't here to scrutinize eyes; he was here to judge whether or not her premises were safe for the public that entered them. If they weren't, he had the power to shut her down. If they were, he was to move on. Simple.

"And the way I operate," he continued, rousing himself, "is by the book."

A "by-the-book" man. She'd already guessed that part herself. Melanie wondered just how long he'd been on the job and what it would take to make him smile. She bet he had a really nice smile if he made the effort.

Her mouth curved, as if to coax a mimicking response from him. Maybe he just needed some encouragement and an example to follow. "And the book says you can't erase a check mark after you made it?"

His eyes narrowed again. "Only if I made it in error."

She placed her hands on the dolly's red handles, her indication clear. All it would take was a few minutes, the time to juggle a little space. "Well?"

Lance knew if he bent the rules for her, he'd have to bend them for everyone. He wasn't about to do that. Besides, in the long run, he was doing her a favor. She couldn't afford to be haphazard when it came to the possibilities of a fire. No one could.

He shook his head. "No error. The check stays. As do these." Moving closer to her, he pointed out several other lines he'd marked off. The scent of something light and airy wafted around him. Was that her, or something in the store, he wondered. There was something very old-fashioned about the scent. It nudged at a memory that was too far removed to catch.

"Where's John Kelly?" Melanie asked suddenly.

"Not here," was the only answer Lance felt she needed to know. "But I am, and you're going to have to deal with the consequences of your flagrant disregard for your customers' safety—and make amends."

He made it sound like an ultimatum. She almost expected him to add, "Or get out of Dodge."

Something egged her on to ask, "Or else what?"

She was challenging him, he thought. Not a smart move. "People who don't follow fire ordinances find themselves shut down."

Melanie stared at him in disbelief. Was he actually saying what she thought he was saying? "You'd shut me down?"

"Not personally, but that would be the upshot."

It wouldn't go that far. Confident that she could handle this to everyone's satisfaction, Melanie indulged the burst of curiosity she was experiencing. It wasn't often she encountered someone so solemn and self-righteous. What was his story? Everyone had a story, and she found herself wanting to know his. He wouldn't give it up easily. He was the type to guard his privacy zealously. She'd always been a sucker for the forbidden.

"Tell me, Lance," Melanie began, and saw a wary look entering the fire inspector's eyes, "what does it take for you to do something personally?"

Chapter Two

The question took him aback.

Was she making him an offer she thought he couldn't refuse in exchange for eliminating the violations? His first answer to himself would have been yes, but there was something in her eyes that made him unsure. Lance didn't know exactly what to make of the woman in front of him, then decided it didn't matter one way or the other. His job description was clear.

In one smooth movement he signed his name to the bottom of the report. Finished, he spared her a glance.

"A lot more than anything I find here," he said tersely, in response to her question. Pulling the sheet from his clipboard, he handed it to her. "I'd see to this fine if I were you."

She was still looking at him as if the fine and the violations that generated them were secondary to her. As if there was something else on her mind, something that, for whatever unfathomable reason, had to do with him.

Maybe it was childish of him, but he'd be damned if he was going to look away first.

"That is, if you don't want to be closed down," Lance emphasized again.

Two women in separate parts of the store turned around immediately. Lance had no idea that he'd raised his voice until one of them asked, "Closing?" Her eyes were almost glowing as she looked around the cozy setting. "Does that mean you're going to be having a closing sale?"

"No, and we're not closing, either." Melanie offered the woman an easy smile. Turning, she shared the smile with Lance. The look he returned was grim. "The gentleman was talking about closing time. We plan to stay right here for a very long time." She gave that assurance to Lance as well as to the customers in the store.

Lance used the interruption to look away from her. He had the oddest, queasiest feeling when she'd been looking at him, almost as if she were offering him sympathy. It was a completely ridiculous idea, but he couldn't seem to shake it.

Lance handed her the citation form. "Then I'd see about those violations if I were you. You have thirty days to get to them." He tucked the clipboard under his arm and turned to leave.

"Does that mean you'll be back?" she asked as he walked away.

"I'll be back," he assured her, though he wasn't looking forward to it, he added silently as he got to the door. Behind him he heard the scraping sound as she pushed the dolly under the stack of boxes.

"I'll be waiting."

She sounded almost cheerful about it, he thought. This

visit obviously hadn't gone well. Why would she welcome another one?

More scraping noise. Somehow, he managed to hear it above the soft music and the low hum of voices in the shop. Lance had an uneasy feeling that he knew what the McCloud woman was up to. Not his business if the slip of a woman wanted to get a hernia or worse, he thought again. The tiny bell overhead tinkled softly as he opened the front door, announcing his exit. The sound seemed to mock him. But he was here to do an inspection, not help her clear away one of her violations. That was the job of whatever poor unfortunate slob she corralled.

Lance liked to think he would have made it out the door if the beveled glass hadn't caught her reflection and flashed it up at him in an almost blinding light. But it did, and his mistake, he realized too late, was to stop and look.

As he'd thought, she was trying to get the dolly under the first pile of crates by herself. Straw had more sense than she did.

For a second he debated leaving her to it, but he couldn't, in good conscience, just keep walking. Aunt Bess had trained him all too well. With a sigh, Lance let the door go and marched back to the annoyingly cheerful woman in the rear of the store.

Melanie could feel a bead of perspiration beneath her bangs as she fought to angle the dolly into position beneath the crates. Another woman would have given up, but another woman wouldn't have wanted to run this sort of shop, either. A place where people came to talk, as much as to buy.

She should have let the delivery man do at least this part of it, Melanie thought, brushing back her bangs before they pasted themselves to her forehead. That's what she got for being softhearted. Not that she really could be any other way. She'd accepted that as part of her nature a long time ago. Some people moved the earth with muscle, others did it with a smile. She chose to take the second path, although she prided herself on being no slouch when it came to strength. She just never muscled in on people, that's all.

Straining, she finally managed to get the platform solidly beneath the bottom crate. Melanie was just beginning to brace herself before attempting to hoist the load when she felt the elbow in her side. It wasn't a gentle nudge, more like an out-and-out takeover.

"Are you out of your mind, trying to do this by yourself?"

The inspector was back, coming to her rescue despite his annoyed question. Melanie tried to suppress the smile that rose to her lips and only partially succeeded. Whoever had named him Lance knew what they were doing.

Lance had taken off his jacket as he'd made his way to the rear of the store and slung it now over the back of a forest green wing chair. With two neat moves, he'd folded up his sleeves.

All her life Melanie had been taught that while people were kinder than they liked you to believe, the best person to rely on in any given situation was herself. She took this approach even with Joy, who was the first to admit that though she was the taller of the two, she was a weakling. This wasn't the first shipment that Melanie had wrestled with on her own.

She shrugged in reply to his reprimand. The man's heart was in the right place, but his attitude needed some fine tuning before it could claim the same thing.

"I'm stronger than I look," Melanie told him.

She was still holding on to the handles. Was he going to have to pry them out of her hands?

Lance looked at her expectantly as his hand covered hers. After a beat, Melanie withdrew hers, that same funny little smile he didn't know what to make of on her lips.

"Harder-headed at any rate," he allowed. "Move out of the way," Lance ordered when she remained standing where she was. "This isn't a two-man job, and even if it were, you wouldn't be one of them."

Obliging him, Melanie raised both hands in a sign of surrender as she stepped to the side. But she was grinning as she did it. "Is that your way of telling me I'm petite and delicate?"

Where had she gotten that interpretation from? Lance wondered. She'd twisted his words into a compliment, when he'd meant nothing of the sort. Although he had to admit, looking at her, that she was both petite looking and delicate. But noting that hadn't been his intent.

He scowled at her. She was making him late for his next appointment. Lance sincerely missed the routine solitude of his work and hoped they'd find a replacement for Kelly soon.

"That's my way of telling you to get out of the way." He could feel his muscles straining as he kept the dolly level and at an angle. What the hell was she thinking of, trying to work this? "You probably hear a lot of that," he couldn't help adding. How had she even managed to wedge the platform under the pile of crate? Glancing at her, he decided that maybe she *was* stronger than she looked. "Where do you want this to go?"

"In the storeroom." Melanie pointed to the back, then realized that he had to know where it was. "But I imagine that you're already acquainted with where that is."

Yeah, he was "acquainted" with her storeroom. "Violations three and four," he muttered, struggling to turn the dolly around. What did she have in this boxes, anyway, anvils? They were a lot heavier and more unwieldy than they looked. If he wasn't careful, the whole stack was going to collapse. Lance didn't particularly like the prospect of getting egg on his face.

Melanie saw the way his muscles were straining as he pushed the dolly. "I really appreciate you stopping to do this for me."

He only grunted in reply, his expression telling her that he didn't think much of her gratitude. Melanie moved in front of him, hurrying to open the door. Holding it with her back, she watched as he pushed the first stack of crates into the room. He accomplished that a lot faster than she would have, she thought.

He looked around for a likely spot. "Where do you want this?"

Melanie left the door open, letting more air in. When he'd passed her, the room temperature had suddenly felt a great deal hotter to her. He was radiating heat, and it left her just the tiniest bit unsettled.

"Wherever I won't get violations five and six," she answered cheerfully, gesturing around the room.

With a dark look Lance angled the dolly out from beneath the bottom box, leaving the pile stacked in the middle of the floor.

"Isn't this violating some code of yours?" she asked, watching him.

"There's nothing wrong with leaving them in the middle of the storeroom," Lance said tersely.

"I mean helping me." Her question went unanswered as Lance returned to the showroom to get the remaining stack of crates. Rather than follow him, she waited until he returned.

He wasn't very talkative, Melanie thought. Not like John Kelly, who enjoyed having an audience and reminiscing about his early days with the fire department.

Melanie watched, with a deep appreciation of the male body, as Lance worked the second and last stack of boxes free of the dolly. He had biceps as hard as rocks, she noted. He also had a deep, long scar running along one of them that became an angry red as he strained. It was too fresh looking to be very old.

She waited until he finished. "Now why wouldn't you let me do that in the first place?"

He had a question of his own. Why couldn't she just accept what he'd done without subjecting it to scrutiny? Annoyed with himself for bothering to help, Lance shoved the dolly away. Unsteady, the dolly tottered like a drunk, then finally clattered to the floor.

"Because that would be favoritism." His eyes narrowed as he looked at her. "I don't believe in favoritism."

She could accept that, she thought as she picked up the dolly and righted it. "But you do believe in being helpful."

"Not particularly." Without bothering to look at her, Lance took down the highest crate and set it on the floor. One at a time, they weren't so bad. For him, he thought. She would have had a hard time of it. It didn't occur to him to wonder what she normally did when a shipment came in. That wasn't his concern.

Neither was this, he upbraided himself, taking down another crate and setting it beside the first.

"You came back to help me," she pointed out. Melanie caught her breath as he swung down a crate from the second stack. "Careful, that one's fragile."

So was she, he thought absently. As fragile looking as the china dolls his aunt kept on display. Setting the box down gently, he realized that was what had teased his mind before. Her store. It was along the same lines of his aunt's dining room. The same kind of furniture. The same subdued scent of vanilla and polish. Maybe that was what had prompted him to help, he thought. That sense of familiarity.

But she didn't need to know any of that. Lance shrugged. "I saw your reflection in the glass door. You looked as if you thought you could tackle this on your own."

It was obvious he thought she was crazy for thinking that. "I could." She waited a beat, then added, "Given time." For his benefit, she flexed a muscle the way weight lifters did and almost succeeded in getting the smile she was after. "I have strong peasant blood running through my veins."

"More like running over your floor if you're not careful. If you get these deliveries in regularly, you should hire yourself a stockboy." He put the last box down on the floor. "Preferably a strong one." He dusted off his hands. "There." Now his conscience was clear, though why it shouldn't have been in the first place still wasn't entirely apparent to him. Lance rolled down his sleeves as he walked out of the storeroom. "See about getting the other violations corrected. And don't be late paying the fine," he warned her.

"Yes, sir."

Lance was certain McCloud was mocking him as she saluted. The dimple in her cheek didn't help his concentration any, either.

On impulse, Melanie looked around before she spied what she was after. "Perfect," she declared, hurrying away.

Lance had no idea what she was talking about, nor did he care. All he wanted to do was leave before she found something else for him to move, push or carry. But she caught up to him before he could make it halfway across the shop. For a small thing, she moved fast.

"Here." She held out what looked like a tiny figurine of a dalmatian wearing a fireman's hat at a jaunty angle, offering it to him.

Lance just stared at it. Now what was she up to? "What's that?"

"It's a dalmatian." How could he not recognize it? Melanie held it up so he could get a better look. "You're part of the fire department, right? I thought it was appropriate."

The smile on her lips seemed to seep into him, like an ink stain, he thought grudgingly. He made no move to accept the gift, not because it could be construed as a bribe, but because he didn't want anything from her.

"I just wanted to say thank you for helping." It was one of her favorite pieces. Impulse had her wanting to give it to him. "It's for luck."

Lance's eyes frosted. Luck. The most highly overrated thing in the world. Where had the old woman's luck been, when he hadn't been able to reach her in time? When she'd died hearing him try to save her?

"I don't believe in luck."

Melanie blinked as he turned from her. She felt as if she'd physically been pushed away. For a second she didn't know what to say. Then she saw his jacket was still on the armchair. She snatched it up and hurried after him.

"Wait."

When he turned around, he found that she'd caught up to him again. She was holding out his jacket. Annoyed at forgetting it, he took the jacket from her and shrugged into it. She was still clutching the ridiculous dog.

Melanie tugged at his sleeve, brushing it off with her other hand. "Lint," she explained, when he looked at her quizzically, pulling away his arm. "Wouldn't want you getting dusty on my account."

Why did her eyes look as if she was enjoying some sort of secret amusement? Lance wondered. And why should he care what she was enjoying, or what she was even thinking, for that matter?

He didn't, he reminded himself. "Just pay the fine," was all he said as he walked out.

In the middle of ringing up a sale, Joy excused herself for a moment and went to Melanie.

"Why did you slip that dalmatian into his pocket?" she wanted to know. Melanie had told her more than once that the piece was not for sale, merely for display. "He said he didn't want it."

Melanie looked at her innocently, though a smile played on her lips. "What makes you think I slipped anything into his pocket?"

"Open your hand," Joy instructed. When Melanie did, it was empty. Joy just shook her head. "I don't think he's the kind of guy who'd enjoy having you practice your sleight of hand on him. He doesn't strike me as the type who likes magic."

"He might not like it," Melanie agreed, looking toward the doorway. "But he's the type who definitely looks as if he needs a little magic in his life."

"Oh, miss..."

Joy flashed an apologetic smile at her customer and hurried back to the register. "You'd think that just being here, selling these things would be enough magic," she said to Melanie. She knew what Melanie was about. There were times when her best friend's heart was just too big for her own good.

One of the other customers beckoned to her. Melanie nodded and went to the woman. "There's never enough magic in the world," Melanie told Joy softly in reply.

Joy merely sighed. There was no arguing with Melanie when she was like this.

His first reaction, when he put his hand into his pocket feeling for his keys and found the figurine, was to turn around and give the damn dog back to her. But that would mean returning to the shop—and to her. And he was reluctant to do that. Lance didn't like facing things he didn't understand unless he was in some way prepared to tackle them. He didn't understand Melanie McCloud or the abject friendliness she seemed so willing to tender. Everyone had a motive, a secret agenda they tried to adhere to. What was hers?

Until he figured it out, he didn't see himself going back there to face that supposedly guileless smile and those blue eyes that looked as if they were fathoms deep.

So he'd kept the tiny symbol of a life that wasn't really a part of him any longer. Kept it until he came into his office and tossed it on his desk where it promptly disappeared into the piles of reports that he had temporarily inherited from Kelly.

He found the figurine again the next day, not that he was looking for it. What he was looking for was the report on the Logan warehouse, a place that had burned down to the ground after being inspected thoroughly only the month before. Supposedly, the fire had been an accident. He still had his doubts about that.

Just as he'd had his doubts about the woman who'd somehow managed to sneak this into his pocket when he'd specifically refused it.

Muttering under his breath, Lance studied the small, foolishly grinning dog. Waste of china, he thought, turning it around in his hand.

The scent of vanilla nudged its way into the cluttered room that usually smelled of sweat and stale air, teasing his senses. Reminding him of her and those improbable dimples that beguiled him.

She was here, he realized. In the station. In his office.

He turned his chair around slowly, as if unwilling to find her there, eating into his space. But find her there he did, standing in the doorway, looking fresher than anyone had a right to be.

He frowned. What was she doing here, anyway? Maybe she'd come about the dog. He wouldn't put it past her to use it as an excuse.

"Something I can do for you?"

He was holding the figurine she'd given him in his hand. She was right, there was a softer side to him. Melanie's mouth curved. "You kept it."

Why did such a simple smile have the effect of a knockout punch on him? The whole thing was beyond ridiculous. Annoyed at his reaction and at her finding him this way, he shrugged.

"I was just about to throw it out." But he continued to hold it.

Melanie merely smiled at the gruff protest. "If you were going to do that, you would have done it when you found it in your pocket." She'd watched him a second before coming in. He'd picked up the dalmatian and looked at it, a sad expression on his face before turning his chair toward the window. What could he have been thinking of that made him look so sad?

No one should feel that sad, or that alone.

Instead of tossing it into the trash, he just dropped the dog carelessly onto his desk. There was enough paper spread all over to pad the fall.

"How did you get it into my pocket?" he wanted to know. He distinctly remembered seeing it in her hand after he'd taken his jacket from her.

It came so naturally to her, she had to stop to remember. "Sleight of hand." The frown on his face deepened. "One of my mother's friends was a magician. My Aunt Elaine put him up at the house for a while when he was down on his luck. He paid her back by teaching me a few tricks."

Sounded like she'd grown up in the middle of a circus. That could go a long way in accounting for her attitude.

"Like coming into a firehouse and trying to get your fines taken care of?" He assumed that she thought she would have another go at him to try to make him change his mind about filing the violations. If so, she was out of luck and too late. He'd filed them as soon as he'd returned, dalmatian in his pocket notwithstanding.

"Already done." She realized he probably thought she'd asked someone to rescind them for her. She could tell by his expression. What had made him so cynical? "I paid them," she added to clear up any lingering doubt.

He didn't understand. Fines were paid at city hall. "Then what are you doing here?"

"Seeing if someone has John Kelly's new address." That had been her original intent, although when she'd walked into the firehouse, she'd asked to be directed to Lance's office instead.

He rocked back in his chair, studying her. He had patience and an eye for detail, which made him a good investigator and the likely choice to fill in for Kelly until they could find someone. But right now, none of that was within his grasp.

"Why?"

Why did he make everything sound like it had to be defended in order to exist? "Because I wanted to send him a gift." She saw the question forming, and answered before it rose to his lips. "He was always nice to me."

In his experience, women who looked like Melanie McCloud were nice to men for one reason and one reason only. "Yeah."

"Like a father," Melanie clarified, wondering whether or not to take offense at what he was clearly implying. She decided not to. He looked as if he was suffering enough as it was. He didn't need someone snapping at him. What he needed, she thought, was someone to listen. And maybe even to care a little. "How dark is the world you're in, Lance?"

He wasn't prepared to have the tables turned on him. With the worn heel of his boot braced against the metal leg of his desk, he shoved his chair back, away from it. It hit against the wall as he rose. He didn't like being analyzed. Served him right for doing a good deed.

No good deed went unpunished, he thought. "It's not dark, it's realistic."

"Then you should understand that a man like John Kelly might just be friendly without compromising his job—or compromising the person he's being nice to," she added significantly.

He'd met Kelly just before the older man had left. A

singularly unimpressive, talkative man with premature wrinkles and yellowing skin from years of being addicted to smoking. They each played with fire their own way, he supposed.

Lance's eyes washed over her slowly, still trying to decide whether or not she was for real. So far, with the exception of his aunt and possibly the mother he just barely remembered, no woman had been. "Did he teach you any tricks?"

There was a point where easy-going just ceased going. Melanie had reached that point. Not for herself, but for the regard, or lack of it, that Lance had for John Kelly, a man she'd truly liked.

Her eyes darkened. "As a matter of fact, he did. He taught me that it was possible to be a fire inspector and not to be a rude, suspicious know-it-all. Otherwise, I would have thought that was what the breed was all about." There was no use talking to him. At least, not until she cooled down a little. "Good day, Inspector Reed. Enjoy your work."

She was almost out the door when he spoke. Part of him was willing to see her walk out. But part of him, some tiny part that sought to justify, to find logic in a world that continued not to have any, pressed him to ask, "You ever see a fire?"

His voice was so low, she almost thought she imagined it. But she turned around, anyway. The expression on his face told her she hadn't imagined the question.

Melanie nodded. "Sure."

He knew exactly what she meant. Lance shook his head darkly. "I'm not talking about something contained within a circle of rocks you roast marshmallows over," he said contemptuously. "I'm talking about a *fire,* something that roasts flesh. That has no respect for who you are or how old you are, it just destroys everything in its path, getting stronger, bigger, defying you to stop it.''

The problem with growing up the way she had, the merest suggestion brought vivid images to her mind. She could see exactly what he was talking about. See it and feel it. Melanie licked her lips before answering. They'd gone completely dry.

"No."

"I didn't think so." Lance kept his distance from her, because he wasn't sure what he would do, just now, if he were close. Shake her or hold her. The latter worried him more than the former did. "I don't enjoy my work, Ms. McCloud. What I enjoy is knowing that if I do my work right, that destructive son of a bitch called fire isn't going to get a chance to get a toehold on the property I inspected." His eyes held hers. "And then no one needs to die."

Melanie blew out a shaky breath as the pain he felt became evident to her.

"How bad was it?" she whispered.

He shook himself free of the memory that haunted him, mentally cursing his lack of control. "What?"

She knew, or thought she knew. "The fire you were in. How bad was it?"

Lance stared at her. Did she profess to gaze into crystal balls, too? "Who said I was in a fire?"

Why did he bother denying it? "*You* did. Not in so many words, but you did."

The sympathy in her eyes unmanned him, sending him to a place he had no desire to be. He didn't have time to waste talking to her. He had work to do.

"Thompson can give you Kelly's address if you're

interested in sending him something. He's the guy look-ing in and staring at you.''

Then, before she could say anything else to him, he brushed past her and walked out.

Chapter Three

"Who's the lady on your desk?"

Her question stopped him cold. This woman seemed to derive pleasure in preventing him from making it through doorways.

Lance turned slowly around. In her hand she held the small, silver-framed photograph of Bess he kept on his desk. The one touch of himself he'd added to an otherwise depersonalized office.

He glared at her. "Does the word *privacy* mean anything to you?"

She'd already begun to put the photograph back, moving aside the pile of folders that had taken the opportunity to spill all over the newly vacated space and obliterate it. His question had her looking at him quizzically.

With a sigh Lance strode back into the office and took the photograph from her. One sweep of the back of his hand and there was room on the desk. He planted the photograph back where it belonged, his eyes warning her to leave it alone.

Melanie looked at the woman with the soft mouth and kind eyes. There was a quiet, serene beauty there that didn't immediately leap out at a person. She raised her eyes to Lance's face. That couldn't be his mother, or else he wouldn't be so touchy about his privacy.

"Why, are you having an affair with her?"

The question stunned him. What kind of mind did this woman have? Were there only photographs of men she'd had affairs with on her desk?

"No, that's my aunt Bess," he snapped.

So, he had filial feelings. There was hope for him yet. Melanie grinned, thinking of her own aunt. "My aunt Elaine never married. Instead she had affairs with younger men. She used to say that was what kept *her* young, and going strong."

Lance couldn't picture Bess having an affair with any man, younger or older. From his earliest recollection, she had been entirely devoted to the memory of her husband, who'd died on a hotly contested piece of dirt half a world away, six months into their marriage. That had been thirty-three years ago. Bess had never shown the slightest inclination of wanting to go out with other men. One heart, one love, that was the way she liked to put it. From the sound of it, that wasn't something Mc-Cloud's aunt would understand.

"Your aunt sounds like a character." Apparently, it was a family trait.

Striving for patience, Lance waited for Melanie to leave. She didn't show the slightest inclination that she was going to.

The grin deepened into a smile. "I suppose she was." Melanie saw the mute question in his eyes when she said *was,* though she doubted he'd ask. Not because any sense of politeness prevented him, but because he

seemed unwilling to accumulate any extraneous information about people. It was almost as if he was afraid
that knowing things would force him to be friendly. She
told him, anyway. "Aunt Elaine died a little over two
years ago. I made the shop look like her parlor."

With all those photographs hanging on the wall? "Big
movie buff?"

He'd asked without thinking. His aunt Bess loved old
movies. They made her sentimental. As a boy, Lance
had watched them with her. Believing in sentiment was
what had set him up for the fall he'd taken, he remembered. His eyes darkened.

Melanie noticed the slight shift and wondered what
brought it on.

"The world's biggest." A fond note crept into her
voice. "That's how she got into her line of work to begin
with. She loved movie stars, loved being around them
and figured she might as well be paid for it."

Lance knew he shouldn't ask. Like leaving food out
for a stray cat, it would only encourage her to stay. But
the same curiosity that made him so good at the inves-
tigations he conducted burrowed forth, obviously not
knowing the difference between being curious about
something trivial and something of grave importance.

"And your aunt was—"

Melanie warmed to her subject, fully aware that he
was leading her out of his office.

"A wardrobe mistress, then a makeup artist for two
of the major studios. She did a bit of designing, too,"
she told him proudly. "Those were some of her clothes
they wore in *Next Year, Paris.*"

Melanie doubted he was even mildly familiar with the
old classic, a tragicomedy that still required at least three
hankies to see the viewer through.

How was it, Lance wondered, with all the people in the world, the world could still be such a small place sometimes? He found it completely uncanny that out of almost an endless selection at her disposal, McCloud would hit upon Bess's all-time favorite movie. Suspicions inched their way forward in his mind, but in all fairness, he had to dismiss them. There was no way the woman could have known something like that on her own. Not unless she knew Bess, and that was highly unlikely. He knew, by sight or at least by name, almost everyone his aunt was acquainted with.

Almost against his will, Lance recalled the first time Bess had made him watch the movie. He was twelve and rebelliously reluctant to sit through what he figured was just a "dumb-old girl movie," though he would have never voiced his protest in those exact words to Bess. But she had prevailed, and he'd found himself struggling not to alternately laugh, then cry, then laugh again. Years later, he figured out she'd probably heard the gurgling noises he'd made and chose, for the sake of preserving his budding male pride, to ignore them and not comment.

Bess was one in a million.

So was the woman with him, for entirely different reasons.

Melanie cocked her head, studying his face. She'd been right. He did look better devoid of that constricting, severe expression he wore. As a matter of fact, he was pretty nearly a heart stopper. She wondered if he knew and decided that he wasn't the type to be aware of things like that.

"You're smiling," she observed, pleased that he did it in her company.

Lance collected himself, lifting his chin as if that would wipe everything away. "No, I'm not."

She wasn't going to let him deny it. There was nothing wrong in smiling. "I'll admit it's not very large, and some might even call it a grimace, but I've been around sound stages. I know the beginnings of a smile when I see one." Her expression teased him, coaxing Lance to deepen the smile. "What?" she urged, wanting to know what had made him forsake that dark, dour expression.

Lance looked at her, debating. Maybe he'd just gotten accustomed to playing his hand too close to his chest, not letting anyone in. Having your teeth kicked in when you most needed someone did that to you.

But McCloud hadn't been the one to do the kicking. In any case, there was no real reason not to tell her. No harm in it, anyway, and then maybe once he told her she would leave him alone and go about her business. Which apparently in her case meant sticking that very pretty nose of hers into other people's lives.

As long as it wasn't his.

He took a chance, shrugging as if it meant absolutely nothing instead of being an incredible coincidence. "It's just that *Next Year, Paris* is my aunt's favorite movie."

Lance wouldn't have admitted that if it weren't true, Melanie thought. Well, well, well. Pleasure poured like rich red wine all through her. "No kidding."

He saw her eyes light up like a child's at Christmas. Why? Bess didn't mean anything to her. She didn't even know Bess.

"No kidding," he echoed.

Lance ushered them out of his office and down the short corridor, very aware that he was garnering looks of unabashed admiration and envy because of his traveling companion. If only they knew. The woman brought new meaning to the term *Superglue*. He'd be more than glad to stick her onto any one of them and get on with his work.

Melanie smiled to herself at his assurance. "No, I don't suppose you know how to do that…kid," she elaborated and ignored the black look from him that followed. He was edging away from her. She took pity on him and began to cut him loose. "Well, you'll have to make a point of stopping by the shop around Christmas. I have a still from the movie autographed by Elliot Anderson. If she's a fan of the movie, I think she'd like to have that."

Bess wouldn't just like it, she'd love it. Lance paused despite himself. Very slowly he blew out a breath, knowing he was going to hate himself for what he was about to say. But this wasn't about him, it was about Bess.

"She has a birthday coming up."

He cared enough about his aunt to make an effort to give her a gift that meant something. The thought warmed Melanie. She was right. He wasn't nearly the bear he wanted her to think he was.

"Even better." She nodded her head, the ends of her hair swinging to and fro over her shoulder. "A birthday surprise. Stop by the shop," she invited again. Then her face brightened. "Or, I can bring the photograph by here if you want."

Lance raised a brow. Just how accommodating was she? He couldn't help thinking that this was still all leading somewhere, to some ulterior motive. Bribery? But that didn't make sense. She'd already paid her fines and besides, none of them had been large enough to warrant bribery to look the other way in the first place. Was there more going on here than he was aware of?

"You deliver?"

She heard the sarcasm in his voice and was determined to take the question at face value only, without offense.

"Sure, why not? It's not as if the fire station is in the next county."

Lance had a feeling that even if it were, she still would have offered.

Though he hated to admit it, it was positively intriguing how one person could be so single-mindedly stubborn about not taking a hint and being on her way.

Lance saw the way Gilhooley was looking at her. The fireman was almost drooling. He thought of asking the man how his wife was, then let it go. Didn't matter to him who the man lusted after, or if the object of his lusting was flattered by the attention.

Still, something almost protective made Lance move so that Melanie was forced to turn her back on Gilhooley in order to face him.

"That's okay," he told her, heading off another unexpected visit from her. "I'll stop by when I get the chance."

"This afternoon if you like. We're open until six-thirty. I'll have it ready for you," she promised. Melanie looked around. There were several firemen and two women in the immediate vicinity. One of them had to be the person he mentioned who had Kelly's new address. "Now which one is Thompson?"

Lance pointed the man out, grateful to be able to finally sic her on someone else.

Melanie slowly cleared off the counter, not that there was much on it to clear. It had been over forty-five minutes since their last customer had left. The hands on the clock directly adjacent to the wall of photographs were inching their way to seven o'clock. The store should have been closed almost half an hour ago.

She supposed he wasn't coming tonight, either.

Joyce eyed her. It wasn't like Melanie to move so slowly. She was usually such a dynamo, just watching her made Joy feel tired. Joy locked up the day's receipts, still eyeing Melanie.

"Is it my imagination, or have you been dawdling about closing the shop the last couple of days?"

There was no reason to make up excuses. "It's not your imagination." Melanie glanced toward the front window. It had an unobstructed view of the street. No cars were slowing down before the shop. "I'm waiting for someone."

"I thought you were meeting your date at the restaurant."

Her date. She'd almost forgotten. In a moment of weakness last week she'd said yes to a friend and had found herself being set up with his cousin, a Wall Street broker visiting from New York. She didn't really feel like going, but a promise was a promise.

Melanie shook her head. "I am. I'm not talking about that."

Joy's interest was immediately aroused. It was beyond her why, with all the things she had to offer, Melanie was still single. "Is he cute?"

Melanie couldn't fault Joy for her matchmaking instincts, though it did get a little old at times. But she knew that Joy just wanted her to be happy. "Yes, but he's a potential customer."

"There's no reason he can't combine the two. Anyone I know?"

"Absolutely." Melanie didn't bother suppressing her grin as she dropped the bombshell. "Inspector Reed."

Joy's eyes widened. "The fire breather?" Was Melanie out of her mind?

Melanie laughed. "That's mostly smoke, I think." She thought of the look in his eyes. There was a soul there, a soul with a great deal of substance. And a great deal of pain. "There's fire, too, but it's not the kind you mean."

Melanie had an incredibly soft heart that led her astray at times, Joy thought. She definitely needed a keeper. Joy pursed her lips, her hands resting in tight fists at her hips. "And you actually invited him to come back?"

"Yes."

Joyce just couldn't bring herself to assimilate the information. There had to be something she was missing. "As a customer?"

Melanie didn't see the problem. "Sure, why not?"

Joy huffed. If they never saw that jerk again, it would be too soon. Didn't Melanie understand that? No, Melanie only understood hurt looks and paws that needed thorns removed from them. Joy shook her head.

"I don't know, maybe we're violating some sort of ordinance or other, and he'll use his 'visit' as an excuse to slap us with another one of his citations. This hasn't been the most lucrative month, Mel."

The reminder didn't faze Melanie. Every down had an up. "It's always a little slow in September, Joy. Next month'll be better."

"So, are you going to linger around here until the Prince of Darkness decides to make an appearance?"

"Maybe just a few minutes." Melanie smiled at the puckered look of concern on Joy's face. "It's not like I have a long way to go in order to get home," Melanie pointed out.

Joy glanced overhead. She was well aware of what

existed upstairs. She'd helped Melanie get it into shape, spending whatever spare time she could find to help paint, scrape and wallpaper. Just like Melanie had helped her the year before.

"No, you don't, I just don't like the look in your eye."

"What look?" Melanie asked. Was she really that transparent?

"Don't play the wide-eyed innocent with me, Melanie McCloud. That look you get in your eyes just before you take in a stray." Melanie might think it was humorous, but Joy saw nothing to laugh about. She placed her hand on Melanie's arm, trying to make her see reason. "Mel, Reed isn't a stray, he's a humorless, angry guy. Good-looking, I grant you, but there're a lot of good-looking guys around. Ones who know how to laugh." Even as she spoke, Joy had a sinking feeling her words were only so many disjointed letters, floating around in a huge bowl of vegetable soup, as far as Melanie was concerned. Melanie wasn't going to listen to anything she had to say. "You don't need a guy with all that excess baggage he's carrying around."

"How do you know what he's carrying around?" Melanie asked, feeling as if someone had to defend Lance. Since there were just two of them in this discussion, it looked as if the job was up to her.

Joyce sighed, knowing the battle was lost. No one stood a chance when Melanie made up her mind. She might look slight, but, like her aunt before her, she had a will of iron.

"You don't look like that and not have something dragging you down. Take my advice, Mel. Close the doors, go upstairs and take a long, hot shower, then put on something slinky and go meet Greg's cousin. Who knows, this could be the start of something big.''

"Maybe," Melanie agreed, but her heart wasn't in it.

"Want me to stay and do your hair?" Joy offered.

She just wanted to guard her in case Lance did show. "Thanks, I'll do my own hair." Melanie placed her hands on Joy's back and gently pushed her toward the door. "Go home to your husband and make your own dreams, Joy. I'll be fine here. I promise."

The expression on Joy's face told her she had her doubts about that.

"I'll see you in the morning," Melanie said with finality.

"I want details about your date," Joy reminded her.

"Right. Details."

Melanie closed the door behind her best friend and let out a long sigh. Then, slowly, she let her eyes wander around the still shop. Alone, it felt different to her. When it was quiet like this, she liked remembering what it had been like, living with Aunt Elaine, listening to the woman's endless stories, basking in her spotlight vicariously.

People were always dropping by the house. People whose faces were recognizable to the general public. People who'd always been just a little larger than life to her.

Melanie had always felt so important because everyone knew Aunt Elaine and, by association, everyone knew her. It had been a great life, growing up with one foot in fantasy, one foot in reality. Melanie had grown up knowing that behind every illusion there was an explanation grounded in truth and the real world. It never ruined the illusion for her, it only made her appreciate it more.

If, every so often, she caught herself wondering what it might have been like to have a father, the next moment someone would pick her up and swing her around, teasing her and calling her their girl. And the lonely feeling would fade away. She didn't have one father, she had half a dozen, doting on her. Caring about her.

She was going to have to see about dropping by the studio again soon, she mused. Things had changed since Aunt Elaine had worked there, but there were still a great many people on the lot who remembered her. It'd be fun to see them again.

Who knew, she might even pick up another batch of memorabilia.

Straightening, Melanie pushed herself away from the door. It looked as if Lance wasn't coming tonight. She might as well get ready for her date. With a twist of her wrist, she locked the door.

Maybe he wouldn't come at all, until the next inspection was due. Too bad. She knew that his aunt would really like the photograph, just like she knew that he needed the conversation, the friendship she could provide.

Her mouth curved as she laughed at herself. There was no fooling Joy. Her best friend had hit it right on the head when she'd accused her of wanting to take in a stray. She'd done that as a kid, Melanie recalled. Only then it had been stray animals with damaged wings and broken legs, desperately in need of care.

Now, she supposed, she was following in her aunt's footsteps, and taking in stray souls who needed more than a full belly and a pillow under their heads to help them get through the night. The full bellies and pillows, that was the easy part. Listening and hearing, that was tricky. Because if you heard, you began to understand what created the neediness.

You didn't have to be poor to be needy.

Just before she pulled down the blinds, Melanie saw the car. It slowed down just in front of the store. Instinctively she knew, though she had no clue what kind of a car Lance drove when he was away from the fire station, that it was Lance. It looked as if he was toying with changing his mind about stopping by.

Not if she had anything to do with it.

Quickly, Melanie flipped the lock again and threw open the door. She hurried out to the curb. "Hi," she called out to him.

His windows were rolled down, and he heard her. And Lance knew that she knew he heard her. Caught, he eased his foot onto the brake, stopping. He should never have come by.

The car idled, fidgeting in neutral.

So was he.

Lance looked at her as she bent down to his window. The breeze saw fit to fill his car with her scent. Everything seemed to be on her side except him, he thought. That made him a majority of one.

"Business so bad you have to stand on the curb and draw the customers in?" he asked drily.

She was getting accustomed to his manner. And immune to it. "Business is fine, thanks. I was just waiting for you."

Seemed to him that she should have better things to do than wait around until he showed up. What if he hadn't shown up at all? He'd certainly considered it. "Why?"

"Because you said you'd be by for that gift for your Aunt Bess."

That struck him as hopelessly naive. Naive people got hurt. It was a fact of life. Didn't she know that? Why did she leave herself open like that? "Maybe I was just making conversation."

He wasn't fooling her. He'd come even though he'd tried not to. Something within him wanted her to reach out to him. If she hadn't thought so before, she did now.

"People make conversation about the weather and baseball scores. They don't talk about fifty-year-old movies unless they have some interest in them."

Lance supposed he had no choice but to park and come in. Either that, or have her talk his ear off right here at the curb.

He pulled up the hand brake. He'd worked late at the station specifically to not give himself this opportunity. It had been his sense of fair play that had him driving by her shop on the way home, just to assuage his conscience that he'd tried without success. He was confident that the place would be closed by then. After two days he didn't figure she'd be sitting waiting for him.

"Don't you close at six-thirty?"

She lifted a slim shoulder and let it fall carelessly. He found himself following the simple movement, taken in by the gentle curves that were involved.

"Generally. But there's no hard-and-fast rule about that. Sometimes I keep the shop open if a customer says he'll be by late." She indicated the second story with a quick sweep of incredibly long lashes. "I live just upstairs so it's no hardship."

He glanced up involuntarily and realized that the windows with the white curtains belonged to her. He hadn't paid any attention to them when he'd been by earlier for the inspection because that had been none of his business. The other woman had clearly told him that the shop was only on the ground floor.

Resigned, Lance got out of the car. "Like to be close to your merchandise?" he asked.

"I think of it as memorabilia, not merchandise," she answered. It was clear by the look on his face that he thought of it as junk, but that was his privilege. She knew better. There were bits and pieces of dreams here. In so many forms. "But in answer to the general intent of your question, yes, I do. I grew up with a lot of it. Being around it keeps Aunt Elaine alive for me.

"C'mon," she hooked her arm through his. "Let me show you what you're getting."

He had an uneasy feeling that she would show him whether he wanted her to or not—and that it didn't strictly involve just the photograph.

Chapter Four

"So, what do you think?"

Melanie set the Florentine eight-by-ten frame on the glass counter and watched Lance's eyes for his reaction. His face was impassive.

She had taste, he had to admit that. The frame she'd selected was delicately understated, the glass purposely nonglare. What stood out was the photograph, a romantic clench between two very beautiful people, and the precise, almost old-fashioned signature on the bottom right-hand corner.

Lance picked up the frame and read the inscription. "To Elaine, with all my gratitude forever, Elliot Anderson." Placing it on the counter again, he looked up at Melanie. "Don't tell me, let me guess. Anderson had an affair with your aunt, too."

Melanie could almost hear Aunt Elaine's bawdy laughter in response to the suggestion. Elliot Anderson might have looked like a dream walking, but it was a dream with a very distinct twist to it.

Melanie bit her tongue, but she couldn't keep a straight face. "Hardly. Elliot Anderson brought new meaning to the term 'a man's man.' He preferred his partners a little, shall we say, more rugged than Aunt Elaine."

"Oh." Lance looked down at the photograph again. Certainly couldn't tell a book by its cover, could you? He reread the inscription and was at a loss as to its meaning. "Then what—"

Melanie obligingly launched into what was one of her favorite stories. "Elliot Anderson had been in a barroom brawl in a scruffy little town south of the border the weekend before shooting *Next Year, Paris* was supposed to begin. *Paris* was touted as being his 'comeback' movie."

Aunt Elaine used to tell the story with much more flair, but Melanie knew that Lance wanted just the bare bones. She trimmed the story as she went.

"Anderson'd had a string of really bad movies, and the studio was going to drop his contract. He really *needed* a hit and *Paris* had all the earmarks of being one. But the director, Simon Backwater, was one of those push-ahead-at-all-costs types. If Elliot wasn't prepared when shooting began, he had someone else in mind. Actually, he was eager to use someone else. He and Anderson hadn't gotten along in years." She saw Lance's impatience and hurried the story along. "Anderson came to my aunt, completely distraught, sure his career and his life were over. With a little polish, a little paint and a lot of skill, she managed to camouflage his bruises well enough to squeak him through shooting until they faded on their own. The rest is history."

But not his, she realized, noting the blank look on Lance's face. She elaborated. "The movie was a hit and

Anderson went on to do very well for himself. He died a star.'' She smiled fondly. ''He always said Aunt Elaine and her 'bag of tricks' as he called them had saved his career.''

The way McCloud told the story, it sounded as if this aunt of hers had been a regular scout leader. Human nature just wasn't like that.

''What did your aunt get out of all of it?''

The question, and the suspicion that had clearly prompted it, caught her off guard. It took her a second to answer. ''Satisfaction.''

The cynic within him didn't believe it. Everyone was always looking out for number one, first and foremost. Hadn't Lauren shown him that, walking away from him when she'd thought she was going to be saddled with a cripple? Even if she hadn't brought the lesson home to him, his father had already laid the foundation. Bruce Reed had walked out on his ten-year-old son because he couldn't deal with the loss of his wife, never once thinking that with that same blow of fate, his son had lost a mother he loved dearly.

Bruce had returned, turning up at his hospital bed after years had passed, but even that was for selfish reasons. He'd only returned in an attempt to soothe his own guilty conscience. Nothing could convince Lance otherwise.

Everyone was out for themselves. Why should McCloud or her late aunt be any different?

Still looking at the photograph, he shrugged. ''If you say so.''

Melanie struggled not to take offense on her aunt's behalf. ''Don't you believe people can do things out of the goodness of their hearts?''

His eyes were steely as he looked at her. ''I don't

believe in goodness, McCloud. It's something that only exists in a kid's fairy tale.''

The amount of hurt Melanie saw just beneath the surface took her breath away. What had happened to this man? How had he become one of the walking wounded? She wanted to know, but there was no one to ask. Yet.

She banked down a wave of pity, knowing he'd snap her head off if he detected it. Instead, she just shook her head. ''And you're related to that nice woman in the photograph on your desk?''

A perverseness he couldn't contain had him challenging her, even though the theories he had about human behavior didn't apply to Bess. They never had. ''How do you know she's nice?''

The answer was simple. ''She has kind eyes.'' Melanie glanced at her watch. It was getting late. Her safety margin was decreasing rapidly. ''Would you like me to wrap this for you?''

Because he wanted to leave, he almost declined her offer, but thought better of it the next minute. He was all thumbs when it came to wrapping gifts. Besides, he figured she'd charge him for it.

''Yeah, might as well. I can't wrap worth a damn.''

Why didn't that surprise her? Melanie smiled to herself as she took out a roll of wrapping paper the color of beaten silver. It complemented the frame. ''Probably because you're out of practice.''

''No one around I want to give anything to besides Bess.'' He missed the sympathetic look in her eyes as he reached into his back pocket for his wallet. She hadn't quoted him a price yet. He glanced at the bills there and wondered if he was going to have to give her a charge card instead. ''How much do I owe you?''

The photograph belonged to the group that wasn't for

sale. Pure impulse had prompted her to offer it to Lance. Even if she tried, she couldn't put a price on it, or the sentiment behind the inscription.

Melanie reached for the tape dispenser, pulling off a piece of cellophane. "Tell your aunt happy birthday for me."

The woman made less and less sense the more he talked to her. Lance didn't see why she'd want him to wish Bess anything on her behalf, but if it made Mc-Cloud happy, it was all one and the same to him.

"Sure," he muttered. "Now how much do I owe you?"

"That's it," Melanie told him, sealing another corner. "Just tell her happy birthday from me. And don't forget to tell her the story I just told you." She could see she was going to have to explain herself. "Aunt Elaine would have wanted that photograph to go to someone who would truly appreciate it. Give it a good home. From what you told me, it sounds as if your aunt can provide it."

The planes of his face hardened, becoming rigid. "I don't accept charity."

He really did make things difficult, didn't he? "Not charity," she insisted. "A gift."

A gift was another name for a bribe. "I don't accept those, either."

Almost involuntarily, he watched her hands as she wrapped. They moved quickly. She had small hands, competent hands. He found himself wondering what they would feel like, moving swiftly like that along a man's body. His body.

What the hell had brought that on?

"Learn," Melanie told him. It was just short of an

order. Then she tempered it. "Besides," she pointed out, "the gift is for your aunt, not you."

That didn't make any difference. A bribe was a bribe and he wasn't about to be put into that sort of position, the way Kelly probably had.

"You don't even know her."

"There's an easy remedy for that. Bring her around sometime," Melanie suggested cheerfully. "I know she'd enjoy herself, and I'd love to meet her." She glanced at her watch again.

That was the second time she'd done that. She didn't strike him as someone who adhered to schedules. "You have to be somewhere?"

"As a matter of fact, I do." Finished, Melanie replaced the wrapping paper under the counter and pushed the dispenser back beside the register. "I'm supposed to meet someone at Land's End on Main in less than half an hour." And if she didn't hurry, she wasn't going to get a chance to change. She still didn't want to go, but if she was going, she intended to look presentable.

"A date?"

Lance looked at her sharply. Had he just said that out loud? From the look on her face, he knew he had. Damn, that had just slipped out.

A date was something you had with someone you cared about, Melanie thought. She didn't even know Bradley Shaffer. He was just in town for a few days, visiting his cousin. It had been her friend Greg's bright idea to get them together.

She'd had a bad feeling about it ever since she'd agreed.

Melanie moved her shoulders in a half shrug. "In a manner of speaking."

He was surprised at the evasive answer. Every other

question had coaxed chapter and verse out of her. Had he stumbled onto a touchy subject? The temptation to pursue it and give her a dose of her own medicine was strong, but that might give her the wrong impression. She's construe his questions to mean he was interested in the answers. He wasn't. All he really wanted to do was get out of the store and go home.

"All done." Melanie held out the package for him. When he didn't immediately take it, she lifted his arm and tucked the package under it. Then she patted his arm into place as if she were handling a mannequin. "There." She stepped back, satisfied. "Tell her to enjoy it in good health."

That was his cue to leave, Lance thought.

So what was he doing, still standing here like some cartoon country bumpkin, his legs and his tongue immobilized by the spark that he saw in her eyes?

It wasn't a spark, it was...

Humor. Was that at his expense? No, she wasn't laughing at him. Not exactly, anyway. He didn't know *what* she was doing exactly, nor, he insisted silently, did he care.

His eyes held hers as he tried not to think how incredibly blue they were. "I told you that I want to pay for this."

He'd stand here all night, arguing with her, if she let him, Melanie thought. Maybe some other time.

With determination she hooked her arm through his and almost pulled him toward the door.

"I'll send you a bill. Right now, I'm in a hurry." Because she'd caught him off guard, she managed to push him over the threshold and out the door.

Closing the door on his surprised face, she flipped the lock. Business hours were officially at an end.

Lance was still standing there, package under his arm, as the lights in the store went out one by one. He had no idea why that generated this incredibly lonely feeling within him.

He backed up on the sidewalk until he could look up at her windows. A couple of minutes passed before the lights came on upstairs. He stood watching, waiting to see a vague outline or a silhouette flirting with the white curtains.

Annoyed with himself, Lance turned on his heel and strode to his car. Careful not to hurt the photograph, he placed it on the passenger side, then got in behind the wheel. He had other places to be.

He was so preoccupied as he drove home he almost went through a red light. Stopping at the last possible moment, the end of his car fishtailing, Lance cursed roundly. It was all McCloud's fault. Somehow she'd managed to slip in through the cracks, to prey on his mind, generating questions he told himself he didn't really want to have answered.

Even the music on the radio made him think of her. Fast, bouncy, catchy. Like her voice and her smile. And the look in her eyes.

Disgusted, he shut it off.

Lance had every intention of going home. There was some leftover Chinese food in his refrigerator that had to be eaten tonight or thrown out. One week was his cutoff point, after that, it was on its way to becoming penicillin. His plans were set. There was absolutely no reason for him to abruptly make a U-turn just as he came in sight of his block. No reason to backtrack until he had driven two miles past her shop and was turning off the engine in his car as it came to a halt in the Land's End parking lot.

No reason in the world except that he was curious. Curious to see what sort of man a woman like Melanie McCloud went out with.

Once he satisfied this bit of annoying, idle curiosity, Lance silently insisted, he'd be on his way. Besides, he'd been meaning to stop by the restaurant. He'd heard two of the men at the station talking about the food here and it sounded as good a place as any to grab a meal.

He didn't really feel like having leftover Chinese food tonight, anyway.

Walking in, he bypassed the hostess with the long, deep burgundy velvet skirt and hundred-watt smile and went to the bar instead. From there he had a clear view of the entrance as well as part of the dining room. If McCloud came here with her boyfriend, he would see her.

The bartender brought him his scotch and soda with a scarlet cocktail napkin and a minimum of dialogue. Lance liked it that way. He'd had his fill of mindless chatter today, even if the voice was melodic.

Sitting back on the stool, Lance sipped his drink and waited for her to show up.

He didn't wait long.

Less than fifteen minutes into his stay, a movement by the door caught his eye, sending his blood pumping through his veins faster than he would have liked to admit.

It was McCloud. She was with a tall, thin, well-dressed man with sharp features and hair the color of toast when it popped out of the machine too soon.

Not bad looking, Lance supposed, in an Ivy League, bland sort of way. Maybe he'd been wrong about her having taste, he mused just before he really looked at her.

She cleaned up nicely, he thought, studying her over the rim of his chunky glass. He'd only seen her in jeans. She was wearing a short, pink dress. One of those straight things that, while not tight, managed to show off every single curve she had. And her legs. He hadn't realized how long they were. She hardly came up to his shoulder, yet from where he sat, she seemed to be all leg.

Suddenly parched, Lance took another long sip. It didn't seem to help.

She didn't look as if she was enjoying herself. But that could have just been his take on it, Lance mused, annoyed that it should matter.

Nursing his drink, he watched as the hostess led McCloud and her boyfriend to their table. It was right in his line of vision.

So he continued looking.

She'd known. As soon as Bradley Shaffer had surprised her and introduced himself at her door, saying something about it being more gallant picking up a woman at her place, she'd known. Known that this wasn't going to work. It didn't *feel* right. She set a lot of store by first impressions.

Bradley might have been Greg's cousin, but he had none of the charm that Greg possessed. And none of the quirky good humor, either. What he did have was a singularly bad case of narcissism. He was in love with the sound of his own voice, the litany of his credits. Within moments he was droning on and on, listing his accomplishments for what she could only think he believed was her astonishment and edification.

By the time the appetizer had reached their table, Melanie had reached her limit. She'd heard, in glowing terms, all about Bradley's incredible business acumen and how grateful his superior was to him for bringing in so many clients to the firm and keeping them satisfied. She wasn't sure she could stand much more.

Deep-set brown eyes looked into hers as if he were trying to hypnotize her. "You know, Melanie, if you put your portfolio into my hands, I can guarantee, right here, right now," he tapped the table with his index finger for emphasis, sending the shrimp into the cocktail sauce, "that when you retire, you will be a very rich woman."

She was twenty-four. Retirement wasn't something that she thought about with any amount of regularity. She supposed someone like Bradley would be appalled by her lack of foresight.

She took a sip of her ginger ale. "Bradley, I don't have a portfolio."

Bradley looked at her as if she'd just told him she intended to throw all her money up in the air and watch the wind scatter it. With dramatic movements befitting a turn-of-the-century Shakespearean actor, he placed his hand over hers on the table and shook his head in abject, galling pity.

"Melanie, Melanie, Melanie, who has been advising you?"

Bradley had managed to do the impossible. His condescending tone had set her teeth on edge. "No one. I—"

If he'd given the indication that he was about to listen, it had been in error. He wasn't going to listen, he was going to take over. And save her from certain impending doom.

"That's very obvious. Lucky for you I came along

when I did. Kismet,'' he added, with what he probably thought was a mysterious smile. He took out a small leather-bound pad from his inside breast pocket and commenced to outline a long-term and, what he assured her was a high-yield, program for her.

Melanie felt her entire body falling asleep. She looked around the restaurant, wondering if there were any exits she could discreetly utilize before she went completely comatose in his company.

When she saw Lance sitting at the bar, she felt her heart literally skip a beat. And then a wide smile followed.

Perfect.

Lance decided there was no point sitting there on the stool, feeling like an idiot any longer. He pushed back his half-finished drink and rose. Sending one final glance in her direction, he saw a look of sheer horror on Melanie's face.

What the hell was wrong? He looked behind him, but there was nothing there. The terror-filled gaze was meant for him and him alone.

Why?

Common sense told him to leave.

But the same iron-fisted curiosity that had urged him to come to the restaurant in the first place had him walking in her direction instead of leaving. He wanted some answers and he wanted them now.

As he approached the table, he saw Melanie's escort turn pale. The man was looking at him as if he'd just walked off the first space ship docking from Mars. Throwing down a handful of bills on the table, he bolted before Lance could reach him.

McCloud's terrified look vanished and dissolved into

laughter as soon as the man's back was turned. Lance waited a beat until she collected herself.

He nodded at her departing date. "Want to tell me what that was all about?"

She took a deep breath and then let it out slowly. If she laughed too hard, she was going to start hiccuping. Melanie looked up at him. Talk about showing up in the nick of time.

"You," she told him. "Living up to your name."

He shook his head, confounded. "Is there some kind of code book somewhere that I should have in order to understand what you're talking about?" Because without one, he hadn't a clue.

"You came to my rescue. Lancelot was always rescuing women." He still looked as if he wasn't following her. "Isn't your full name Lancelot?"

Lance pressed his lips together. He would have been better off following his first instinct and just walking out of the restaurant. With a sigh, he nodded. He didn't readily like to admit to the name written on his birth certificate. The choice, he was told, had been his mother's. It was something that had earned him more than one black eye as a kid. It had been years since anyone had dared call him that.

His mouth remained hard, unsmiling. "I don't see what that has to do with your fleeing boyfriend."

"He's not my boyfriend." That, she thought, would have been a fate worse than death. "He was a blind date I agreed to go out with because I'm a pushover where my friends are concerned." She could see she'd lost him again. "Bradley Shaffer is in town from New York, visiting his cousin. Greg asked me to show him around."

Greg, he assumed, was the friend who'd turned this headstrong woman into a pushover—not that he believed she was one for a minute. If she did anything, it was because she wanted to.

"And?" he asked, wanting to find out why the man had looked at him as if he was some homicidal maniac.

She motioned to the chair Bradley had all but knocked over in his haste to leave, but Lance remained standing.

"He was about to create a retirement portfolio for me, making it in his image and likeness." A mischievous smile played on her lips. "He was putting me to sleep," she confided.

Lance tried not to notice that her smile was having an unsettling effect on his stomach. He wrote it off to the fact that he hadn't had dinner yet and those were hunger pangs he was experiencing, nothing more.

"Maybe that's how he gets women into his bed," Lance commented. Impatience drummed at him with bony fingers. The woman didn't know the meaning of getting to the point. "But I still don't understand why he ran out like that. He looked really afraid of me."

"He was." Pausing, Melanie wondered how he'd react to this. "I told him you were my ex-boyfriend. My very jealous ex-boyfriend who had come looking for me." She watched his eyes. "I said the last man you found me with was still listed by the police as missing." Melanie toyed with her glass of ginger ale, pleased with herself. "I guess he decided my portfolio wasn't worth dying for."

That explained the man's reaction, but not hers. "You looked really terrified."

"I had to convince him," she explained, then added, "can't hang around sound stages without picking up a few things." Since he wasn't quick on the uptake, she decided to stop being subtle and invite him outright. "Have you eaten?"

He answered before thinking of the consequences his answer had. "No, I—"

"Perfect." Leaning over, she moved the chair out for him. "Let me buy you dinner. You did me a big favor by rescuing me."

He wasn't about to have her get carried away with this. God only knew where that would lead. "All I did was walk toward you, you're responsible for the rest of it."

"You were in the right place at the right time." She looked at Bradley's jumbo shrimp cocktail. He hadn't touched it. "It's a shame to let this appetizer go to waste."

Against his better judgment, Lance remained. He knew he was in trouble the moment she turned her smile on him.

Chapter Five

"Do you come here often?"

Lance stopped pulling his chair in and looked at the woman seated across from him. "What?"

Melanie repeated the question as innocently as before. "Do you come here often?"

Seated, he scrutinized her face. Was that her rather unsubtle way of asking if he had specifically come to the restaurant looking for her?

"No, why?"

For a second Melanie had actually thought he was finally going to stop being defensive. It was going to take a little more time before that happened. She was willing to wait.

She lifted one shoulder, letting it fall casually again. He was watching every movement as if he was looking for a clue to some great puzzle she was unaware of.

"I thought if you did, maybe you could recommend something on the menu." Melanie looked at him over the flickering candle on the table, watching the way the shadows played along the planes of his face. "I've never been here before."

Feeling a little foolish now, Lance lowered his eyes to the aqua-colored menu that lay, unopened, beside his appetizer. "Sorry, can't help you."

This, too, she shrugged away. "Well, you've done enough for me for one night. Maybe even for a whole month."

He regarded her with suspicion. Just what was she getting at? Did she think because he was sitting here with her right now that they were on the verge of some long-term relationship? One that lasted longer than the time it took to finish a meal? It seemed improbable, but he'd already learned that she had her own way of thinking.

Finding that she had an appetite after all, Melanie took a bite of her shrimp cocktail and savored the taste before continuing. "Bradley sounded as if he was prepared to completely reorchestrate my life by the time the evening was over."

By any standard Melanie McCloud was an attractive woman. Maybe even beautiful, as long as she kept her mouth shut. It didn't make any sense to him. "Why did you do it?"

Though she was pleased that he was actually initiating a conversation, she wasn't sure what he was referring to. "Do what?"

"Agree to go out with that creep." Even as he asked, Lance told himself it was none of his business what she did or with whom. He also realized that he'd slipped when he called the man a creep. There was nothing to base the judgment on, other than a gut feeling. He wasn't supposed to be having gut feelings about her.

Her mouth curved in that funny way of hers, as if she

were sharing an amusing secret with herself, daring him to guess what it was. Lance found it difficult to concentrate on what she was saying.

"I didn't exactly agree to go out with 'him,' I agreed to go out with Greg's cousin."

Had he missed something? "But Shaffer is Greg's cousin."

She looked at her appetizer and saw that she'd managed to eat the whole thing without realizing it. Being rescued certainly made her hungry. "Right."

She'd lost him again. He began to wonder if it was possible to have a conversation with her without feeling that way.

"And the difference between going out with Bradley and going out with Greg's cousin would be—" Lance waited, defying her to make sense out of this.

Moving the empty glass aside, Melanie patiently explained. "If I'd agreed to go out with 'him,' that would have meant that I liked Bradley. If I agreed to go out with Greg's cousin, then I was doing Greg a favor."

He supposed that made sense, in a sideways, off-beat sort of way.

"That's a very unique piece of logic. I'm surprised some university hasn't snapped you up in order to conduct a long-range study on elliptical reasoning."

He was capable of humor. She liked that. Melanie raised her eyes to his face. It had softened a little. She liked that, too.

"Are you offering?"

Back to the land of the lost, he thought. Didn't take long. "Offering what?"

"To study me," she prompted.

There was an invitation in her eyes, one that was

tempting him despite all his best resolutions. "Why? Would you say yes?"

"I might." Her mouth curved again. How would that mouth feel, curving under his own? He wanted to find out more than he knew he should. "A lot sooner than I would have said yes to Bradley." She paused, as if weighing her words, then said, "Yes."

The word sizzled between them, waiting for a response. Lance's mouth felt dry as he forced the words out. "I'll keep it in mind if I ever get a grant."

He saw the waitress approaching their table. She looked obviously surprised that McCloud's dinner partner had changed. Her bewildered expression amused him. *Welcome to the club.*

Opening the menu, Lance skimmed the two sides, trying to remember what Thompson had mentioned he'd enjoyed when the firefighter had eaten here. He found it on the second side and asked the waitress for a serving.

"Make that two." Closing her menu, Melanie handed it to the woman. Lance raised a questioning brow. "I trust your judgment," Melanie explained as the waitress walked away. "Besides, I'm easy."

Was she? Lance wondered. Was she "easy"? And just how easy was easy? He knew she was certainly easy on the eyes, growing progressively more so with every passing minute. The more he saw of her, the more he liked what he saw. Which, Lance upbraided himself, he shouldn't allow to become a habit.

"Don't let that get around," he commented, as if whether she did or not was really a concern of his. What did it matter to him if people, if men, thought she was easy. She was no one to him.

And he intended it to remain that way.

She laughed softly, the low, throaty sound going right

through him, landing in his gut. Disgusted with his very physical reaction, Lance attributed it to the scotch and soda.

"Why not?" she asked. "I think life's too complex as it is. Some things should be easy. Talking, making friends—"

Her statements were far too blanketing for his liking. "Acquaintances," he corrected, contemplating the last jumbo shrimp in his cocktail glass. He didn't much care for the taste. Lance saw the way she was eyeing it and decided that the shrimp might as well go to someone who would appreciate it. He held it out to her. "Making acquaintances is easy, at least for someone like you."

To his surprise she didn't take the fork. Instead she took his wrist, holding his hand steady as the last bit disappeared between her lips. Stirred, he had to concentrate hard to remember what he was saying. "Making friends is another matter altogether."

Slipping her fingers from his wrist, Melanie sat back again. "Not really, not if you leave yourself open."

His pulse was unsteady, he thought in annoyance. Served him right for having that drink. It was much too strong for an empty stomach to handle properly.

And her words were much too soppy for his stomach to handle, he thought. Her sentiment was hopelessly naive. "If you leave yourself open, someone is liable to walk all over you with very muddy shoes."

He said that with much too much conviction, Melanie thought. The teasing note left her voice as she leaned forward again, her attention riveted to the man sitting across from her. For the briefest moment she saw the sadness in his eyes before the curtain dropped again.

"Did someone?"

The sympathy she was silently offering made him uncomfortable. "Did someone what?"

She had her answer in his tone, she just didn't have the specifics. "Walk all over you with muddy shoes?"

Did she take some sort of perverse pleasure in always turning things around? "We were talking about you," he reminded her tersely.

He'd slipped, Melanie thought, and given her a glimpse into his world, into his pain. For now, she pretended not to notice. He didn't trust her enough to share yet. But he would.

"Well then, no," she answered, "no one has. And I have a lot of friends to show for it."

"Lucky you." He couldn't help the sarcasm that spilled over.

"Yes." Her eyes held his and he realized that she was deadly serious. "Lucky me. Do you have a lot of friends?" Were there people in his life who meant something to him besides his aunt? People he might be shutting out for some reason? Questions began to multiply in her head.

He gave her a black look. It was an absurd question. "No." He'd been a loner for as long as he could remember. Even before his father had walked out on him. That was why the wounds Lauren left behind had gone so very deep. Because he'd opened himself up to her, trusted her. Loved her.

And been a fool.

Melanie believed him, and the emptiness was almost too much to bear. "Well, you have me."

Did she really think it was that easy? "We're not friends," he pointed out gruffly. "We barely know each other."

Oh, but I know you, Lance. I know the pain you're feeling and I want to make it better.

Her smile was warm, gentle. How could there be so many facets to just a simple curving of her mouth, he wondered, trying not to let himself be drawn in.

"Now, there you're wrong," Melanie contradicted cheerfully. "I know what you do for a living and where your office is. I even know your aunt's favorite movie." She knew just what his comeback to that would be and headed him off. "And as for me, you can ask me anything you want."

His eyes narrowed. Couldn't she take a hint graciously? "And what if I don't want to ask you anything?"

Melanie merely smiled as she sipped her drink. "Oh, but you will."

He wanted to deny it, but he had an uneasy feeling that she was already right.

But the kinds of questions he wanted to ask her would only lead to trouble, and he wasn't in the market for trouble. He wasn't in the market for friends, either, but she seemed to be determined to be his. He couldn't understand why that seemed so important to her.

Lance pointed to the amber liquid in her glass. It was almost gone. "If you ask me, you've had too much to drink."

She grinned, her eyes dancing wickedly. "I almost never get high on ginger ale."

"Ginger ale?" he echoed. He'd assumed that she was drinking white wine. The waitress had served it in a wineglass.

"Ginger ale." Melanie held the glass up to him to inspect. Lance held up his hand, refusing it. She set the glass down on the table. "But life, however," she continued, "well, I get high on that all the time."

Was she for real? A part of him almost wished she was, but he knew that was impossible. Nobody was this uncomplicated and still functioning in the world. "There's a word for people like you."

"Yeah, I know—*optimist.*"

"I was thinking of *nuts.*"

She looked into his eyes and then laughed. "No, you weren't. The word that occurred to you was probably a lot more potent than that. Am I right?"

"Yeah." Stymied, Lance threw back the rest of his drink. It went down, smooth as silk. As smooth as he figured her skin would feel when he touched it.

If, he amended, not when. *If* he touched it. Which he wasn't planning to.

The hell he wasn't.

She was scrambling his brain, he thought darkly. He didn't need this. "You're right." It was as if she could read his mind. "And just how did you arrive at that conclusion? Is this some 'divine' power you have, or have you just driven a lot of people nuts?"

It had nothing to do with her effect on him, it had to do with what she could see in his eyes, Melanie thought. What she could hear in his tone. Nuances were very important in the world she'd come from. "I've been around a lot of people in my life. You can't help getting good at reading them after a while."

"You can if you ignore them." Ignoring everything around him except what related to his work was second nature to him. And comforting in an odd way. But he still didn't miss the fond note that entered her voice and found himself wondering just what sort of childhood she'd experienced, growing up the way she had.

She folded her hands in front of her and leaned her cheek against the linked fingers, studying him. Wishing he could trust her. "That's the difference between us right now, Lance. I like people."

He picked up on her phrasing. "What do you mean, 'right now'?"

"Just what I said. I think at bottom, you're like me. Something just got in the way." She believed that with her whole heart.

"Common sense." One of the first lessons he'd been taught as a firefighter was to know when to get out of a burning building before it collapsed. It was time to get out. "And common sense says I should be going." Pushing his chair back, he began to rise.

He felt the light pressure of her hand on his, felt the electricity as it passed from her to him, a hundred-pound woman stopping a one-hundred-eighty-two-pound man cold in his tracks.

"Stay." The word whispered along his body more gently than a caress. He struggled to ignore its effect. "We've already ordered, and I hate eating alone."

He looked at her, leaving his hand trapped where it was. "You're not alone. You're surrounded by all these people." He nodded at a table. "Why don't you go and make them your friends?"

She knew what he was doing. Trying to push her away, to make her angry enough to give up. She wasn't about to let him get to her. Not on that level. On a different level, he already had. He'd stirred her compassion to a high point. "I'd rather concentrate on making you my friend."

He read things in her eyes, things he didn't believe in. Things he told himself he was only imagining.

Women like Melanie didn't exist. They were an illusion, created by a mind that needed to believe.

"Why?"

She told him honestly. He wouldn't have accepted anything less. "Because I think you need one. A good one who'll listen."

What gave her the idea he'd bare his soul to her? "I'm not talking."

She looked into his eyes. "Not with your mouth." A movement in the distance caught her eye. "Look, our dinners are coming." He still looked as if he was going to leave. "I promise, for the remainder of the meal, I'll be good. We'll talk about anything you want to talk about."

"And if I don't want to talk?"

She lifted her shoulders, letting them fall beguilingly. "Then we'll eat."

Yeah, like he really believed that. Still, he didn't have any other place to be, and the leftovers in his refrigerator had probably turned by now.

He made up his mind. "Fair enough, I guess."

Melanie only smiled. One battle down, a hundred to go.

She'd lied.

To be fair, she did try to keep her word. She did try to let him lead the conversation. Except that he didn't, preferring to see how long she could hold out. By his watch, she'd struggled with herself a full five minutes, maybe five and a half, before finally breaking down and talking.

If he were being totally honest, he had to admit that he didn't mind all that much. Listening to her talk, as long as the conversation didn't center on him, was like listening to the music made by those early-morning birds he remembered hearing when he and his father used to go fishing.

The memory caused him to pull up abruptly, his breath catching. He hadn't thought about that in years. Hadn't thought about all those summers he'd gone fishing with his father.

But even as he tried to push the memory away, it refused to leave. Instead it came at him from all sides, squirming in through the gaps. Bringing with it a bittersweet feeling he didn't want.

His mother, getting up early Saturday morning and pretending to grumble as she made sandwiches for his father and him, sending them both off into the predawn darkness with a warm thermos of soup, a basket of sandwiches and a dose of love.

He and his father, sitting on that damn, rocking rowboat for hours, watching the sunrise over the lake and, like as not, catching nothing.

Sunrises on the lake were so beautiful, the center of his chest used to ache just looking at them.

He felt an ache now, but it was a different sort of ache. It was the kind of ache you felt when you knew something was dead.

It was dead. All that had happened to someone else. Someone else who knew what it was like to believe in happiness going on forever.

Someone who wasn't him.

His expression was stony. Melanie set her fork aside. "Oh, God, I've bored you to tears."

Snapping out of it, Lance looked at her. She'd said something, but he hadn't heard. "What?"

"You drifted off." A self-deprecating smile lifted the corners of her mouth. "Was I really that bad?"

"No." He shook himself loose of the memory's grip. It wasn't easy. Bits and pieces had woven themselves into his consciousness. "I was just thinking about something, that's all."

Not just "something." He'd gone almost pale. Melanie knew he wouldn't appreciate her pointing that out. She swallowed the temptation to ask.

The waitress approached with the bill, and Melanie took out her charge card, ready to place it on the small silver tray beside the itemized statement.

He caught her hand before she could reach up to do it. "What are you doing?"

She looked at Lance in surprise. "Paying for the meal."

"Put that away," he growled. Releasing her wrist, he fished out his wallet.

"But I told you, dinner was on me." They'd already discussed it. Or rather, she'd made the offer in order to get him to stay. But he hadn't refused.

"Put that away," Lance repeated.

She didn't want to argue with him and spoil what was left of the evening. Despite his reluctance to remain, she'd had a really nice time...and made, she hoped, just the tiniest bit of headway.

"Okay. Thank you." Tucking the card back into her wallet, she quickly fingered the bills she had there, mentally counting them. "I can always use some of the money to pay for the fare."

"The fair?" Now what was she talking about? Was there some fair in town she was going to try to drag him to?

"Yes." Still counting the ones, she didn't look up. "For the cab."

She wasn't talking about a fair, she was talking about

cab fare. It still didn't make any sense to him. "What cab?"

Melanie closed her wallet and deposited it into her purse. "Well, my ride home is probably halfway back to New York by now. I have to get home somehow."

He'd assumed that she'd driven here in her car. "I thought you said you were meeting Shaffer in front of the restaurant."

"I was supposed to," she agreed, "but there was a slight change of plans. Bradley insisted on picking me up at my apartment. When he arrived, he wanted to spend a little 'quality time' with me before coming here." She touched the tip of her tongue to her lip, and Lance wondered why he found that so impossibly sexy. "That was the first inkling I had that this was not going to turn out to be the date of the century."

She was being awfully cavalier about the situation. The slime might have tried to force himself on her. Didn't she think of these things? "What were you going to do when he took you home?"

She'd had that all figured out by the time they arrived at the restaurant. "Run like crazy and lock the door behind me before he could get to it."

He could see her doing it, too. He didn't realize he was smiling when he told her, "Save your money. I'll take you home."

She would like that, she knew. But she didn't want him to feel obligated. "You don't have to."

He got up, one hand on the silver tray, one hand on her arm. He took charge of both. "McCloud, shut up. I said I'm taking you home, and I'm taking you home. Now that's the end of it."

"Yes, sir."

Right, like she would dutifully accept anything, he thought darkly, walking to the hostess desk with her.

But it wasn't the end of it. It was just the beginning. Lance had that sinking feeling even before he pulled up in front of her shop. Even before he walked her to her door. This wasn't going to be the end of it, even though it should be. Why wasn't he turning around and leaving?

She didn't have to fish for her keys. She knew just where they were. On a ring attached to the inside of her purse. For the moment she left them there as she turned her body into his and looked up at him.

"Would you like to come up for a few minutes?"

The moon was out, and with it more stars than he ever remembered seeing. The street, so busy during the day, was almost eerily quiet as he stood there with her. The cool breeze he'd unconsciously expected hadn't materialized. Instead, there was a warm one in its place. Warm, like the feel of her breath along his throat as she asked the question.

Yes, he would, he thought. He would like to come up. More than that, he wanted to stay the night.

That was just the damn trouble.

No, she was. She was trouble with a capital *T.* Lance knew when to draw the line in the sand. He just hoped he had the good sense not to cross it.

Still, he wasn't moving toward his car, wasn't leaving. He was scarcely even breathing. "You're not going to run like crazy and lock the door?"

Slowly, her eyes on his, she moved her head from side to side. "You haven't given me any reason to."

But she'd given it to him, he thought. Lots of reasons

to run like crazy and lock the door to keep her out. And himself in.

"I'd better go," he muttered.

She didn't want him to go. She wanted him to stay. But she didn't want him doing anything he didn't want to do, either. It wouldn't count then.

"Thank you for rescuing me. I had a much nicer evening than I thought I would when I first left the house."

There was just enough light to play off her skin, making it silvery. His knees were doing strange things. He wanted to touch her. "Doesn't take much to please you, does it?"

They were standing close, so close that she could almost feel his heart beating. Could feel the heat of his body whispering to hers. "Like I said, I'm easy."

Yes, he thought, she was. Easy. Very easy to allow under his skin.

Before he could think and stop himself, Lance wove his fingers into her hair.

He was right, it did feel soft.

Would he be right about her mouth as well?

And then, though he knew it was a mistake, a mistake he was going to regret, a mistake he was destined to make, Lance framed her face with his hands and brought his mouth down to hers.

Chapter Six

Softly, like the reverent whisper of a child at prayer, Lance's lips moved slowly over hers.

He could hardly believe he was doing this, kissing Melanie when he had tried so hard to be firm, to hold himself in check.

And away from her.

What the hell was he thinking?

That was just it, he wasn't thinking. He wasn't thinking at all, only feeling. Only reacting. And enjoying. God help him, he was like a man having his first glass of water after an interminable drought. He didn't know whether to sip it, gulp it or drench himself with it.

What he couldn't do was walk away.

Tilting her head, his fingers lightly skimming the sensitive skin along her throat, Lance deepened the kiss. Deepened it until he lost himself in it, a militant lost in the heat of battle.

If he was reluctant to surrender, it was merely a moot point. He was already gone.

His body surrendered for him, allowing him to be taken prisoner by these sensations that were battering at him so insistently. She made his head swim, his blood heat and his body yearn for a time when he could just lose himself in a woman and not think of consequences.

Anticipation had zipped through Melanie like a heartbeat before she felt his lips touch hers. Anticipation told her what to expect. After all, it wasn't as if she hadn't been kissed before.

She hadn't.

Not like this.

Anticipation, grounded in the past, hadn't begun to prepare her for what lay immediately ahead. It was like riding a tricycle in preparation for a motorcycle, or being on a merry-go-round in preparation for mounting a wild mustang. There was absolutely no comparison between what had once been and what now was.

And what it was, was wonderful.

On her toes, trying to steep herself in the feel of his mouth and the warmth of his breath as it cascaded along her skin, Melanie wound her arms around his neck, her body around the fire that was licking at her from all sides. Wound herself around it and gave herself up to it. Willingly.

The groan of pleasure came from somewhere deep within her. With all of Hollywood's magic at her feet, she'd still never known, never dreamed, that kissing a man could feel like this.

Like sunshine bursting in her veins.

He tasted her moan within his mouth. His blood pumped harder, setting a torch to his excitement. The flame rose higher.

If he wasn't careful…

He wasn't careful, that was just it. He'd slipped and let the last kernel of need within him heat until it popped.

With effort, though everything within him screamed out against it, he drew away.

Melanie blinked, trying to focus. Her bearings were all blurred. She slipped her hands automatically to his shoulders to steady herself. How was it that she'd managed to remain standing when her kneecaps had been vaporized?

Looking up, all she saw was Lance. It was all she wanted to see.

"Wow."

He laughed, then. He didn't mean to, and there was nothing funny about what he'd just allowed himself to do, but he laughed at the startled, disoriented look on her face. She looked beyond pretty, beyond beautiful.

She looked adorable. And completely irresistible.

And then he did something even more incredibly stupid than when he'd first kissed her.

He kissed her again.

His lips hungrily devouring hers, Lance took Melanie into his arms with an urgency that he no longer was foolish enough to believe could be controlled. This kiss wasn't exploratory. This kiss came from a man who was hungry, who wanted. Who'd lost and believed he would keep on losing.

It was almost savage in its neediness.

Melanie felt herself being sucked into a vortex. At first there was a flash of blinding panic, a desire for survival. But it was gone almost before it came. There was nothing to be afraid of. She wanted this, wanted him.

She went into the vortex without a struggle, memorizing every sensation, every texture she encountered with what was left of her brain.

She'd never felt so wanted, so needed before in her life. She knew she never would again, not with any other man.

His hands were molding her against him, brushing along the length of her, sealing her to him until it was difficult to know where one of them ended and the other began. She didn't want to know, because it was all one and the same.

Melanie had never realized until this very moment that there had been something missing from her life. Now, for the first time, she felt completely whole.

Lance felt a thin blade of panic wedge its way through the fire, carving a path along his belly. If he didn't stop now, he was going to take her. Take her here and now and make love with her all night.

And in the morning, when light shattered the fantasies created in the secret of shadows, he would leave and not come back. Because he couldn't. Couldn't return, knowing that disappointment would inevitably claim him.

Every good moment exacted a payment. Every good moment was paid for with days of pain. He knew that, had lived through that. The next time he might not make it.

He had to go and go now.

Her warmth made him want to stay.

She was trembling, he realized slowly, his brain still drugged with the very essence of her. She was shaking against him like a leaf tossed in the wind.

Had he frightened her? He didn't want to frighten her, but he must have. Because he sure as hell had frightened himself.

Lance drew his head back, trying to quiet the pounding in his veins, in his head. Concentrating, he focused on her face. His heart twisted within his chest. Her lips were a little swollen.

He cursed himself inwardly. She probably thought he was some kind of animal.

Lance dragged air back into his aching lungs, wishing he could just go away and not look back. But he couldn't go, not without saying something. He owed it to her.

He skimmed his finger along the hollow of her cheek, where a faint discoloration mocked him. His fingers had pressed there as he'd framed her face.

Lord, it was as if he didn't even know himself. "I didn't mean to do that."

"It's a little late for apologies." Gingerly Melanie touched her fingers to her lips. She could still feel him. Still taste him when she pressed her lips together. Talk about being overwhelmed. "Is this what it feels like to be branded?"

It took him a moment to realize that she wasn't angry. He'd lost his head and his cool and all but groped her in her doorway and she wasn't angry. She was making a joke of it.

What kind of woman was she?

Lance looked into her eyes and had his answer.

Except he didn't believe what he saw, refused to believe that she was good and pure and willing to take him, scars and all. He was sharp when it came to his work, at the top of his game when it meant investigating fires. But he'd lost faith in all his senses when it came to dealing with women. His judgment was impaired. He'd been wrong before, why shouldn't he be wrong now?

Waiting for his pulse to stop beating erratically, Lance dragged an impatient hand through his hair. He didn't want her thinking things. That maybe he felt something for her. That maybe this could go somewhere. Because it couldn't.

"Look. What just happened here...it shouldn't have." He slanted a glance at her face, waiting to see the anger. He could deal with anger, was equipped to deal with anger, his own and anyone else's. It was kindness he didn't know what to do with. Like the kindness he saw in her face. "I'm sorry if I hurt you."

He'd scared himself, Melanie thought. He'd felt something, just as she had, and he'd scared himself. Here was a man who was going to have to be led, gently, slowly and with patience. She didn't mind. She was up to it.

"You'll only hurt me if you apologize again." She smiled at him, surprised she could still make her lips work. "You only kissed me, Lance, you didn't declare war or sack me."

In the midst of his inner turmoil, she made him pull up short. What the hell was she talking about? "Sack you?" he echoed.

Amused, she nodded. "Like the Vikings did when they overran countries, robbing and pillaging." Her smile teased him. "What's the matter, didn't you ever see that movie with Kirk Douglas and Tony Curtis?"

The ache he was struggling against was too dark, too wide for him to be teased out of.

"No," he snapped. "I didn't. And I had no business kissing you."

There was guilt in his eyes. "Is there someone else?" she asked. She hadn't thought there was, but maybe she'd made a mistake. Melanie held her breath.

"Yes."

She felt as if someone had shoved ground glass into her palms. He was married. She'd just kissed and given her soul away to a married man. The thought devastated her and sent her reeling.

"Oh."

Because she looked so crushed, he decided he'd tell her...at least a part of it. That, too, he figured he owed her. "An old woman who died in a fire."

Then, he wasn't married. Her brows furrowed. What did the woman have to do with what just happened now between them? "I don't understand."

He didn't want to talk about it. It was enough that it had gutted his insides when it happened. That he still woke up in the dead of night, hearing her scream. But he'd opened this door and now had to close it somehow.

Consider it payment for a moment of rashness, he thought, looking at her mouth.

"She died thinking I would save her." The shrug was as angry as it was helpless. "I didn't."

But he had tried, she thought. He'd tried very, very hard. "Is that how you got your scar?" Lance looked at her sharply. She could tell she'd guessed correctly. Her heart went out to him. "You took off your jacket and rolled up your sleeves when you helped me move the crates the other day. I saw a scar on your arm. It looked fresh."

"Two years," he told her. The scar, the memory, all of it was two years old. He felt like it had happened yesterday.

"You were a firefighter?" It wasn't really a guess. Melanie knew the answer before he nodded. "What happened?"

Why was he telling her all this? He didn't want to remember, and he certainly didn't want to share something like this with anyone.

Tension made his jaw rigid. "The building was on

fire. I couldn't reach her in time. She died. End of story, all right?'' He was shouting at her and hating himself for it.

She looked beyond the angry eyes that were cutting her to ribbons. This wasn't about her. This was about him, and the hair shirt he was making himself wear.

"No, it's not all right," she told him gently. "Not until you forgive yourself."

"That would be too easy," he said, turning away.

"No—" her voice followed him as she walked to his car "—from what I see, that seems to be the hard part."

He got in and drove away, never looking back.

Melanie watched the car disappear from view before she finally went inside.

Joy waited for what she thought was a decent interval of time. She gave Melanie exactly fifteen minutes from the time she walked into the shop before she launched into the question that had been nibbling away at her.

Cornering her at the register, Joy asked eagerly, "So, how did your date go?'

Melanie had thought about him all night, wondering what it must be like, feeling responsible for someone else's death. She couldn't begin to imagine. What she did know was that in his case, the guilt was unjustified. She believed that with every fiber of her being.

Preoccupied, Melanie mechanically placed bills into the proper slots in the register. They'd be opening for business within five minutes. "Fine, until the end."

Joy tried to read her friend's expression to no avail. "What happened?"

Melanie closed the cash drawer, leaning an elbow on the counter as she remembered and relived. "He kissed me until I thought my toes would burn a hole through my shoes and into the concrete, and then he left.''

That didn't sound right to Joy. That sounded like a prelude to a romantic night, not an evacuation. Something must have happened that Melanie wasn't telling her. "For no reason?"

There was a reason, all right. But not the right one. Melanie crossed to the rear wall and frowned. They'd sold several photographs in the past few days. She was going to have to rearrange them until she found more to fill the empty spaces. "It had something to do with a woman he couldn't save from a fire."

"A fire," Joy repeated, confused. "I thought Greg's cousin was a stockbroker."

Looking for the notebook she kept her current records in, Melanie moved back to the front counter. "He is."

It would help, Joy thought, if she didn't have to talk to a moving target.

"Then what—" Staring at Melanie's back, Joy had a horrible thought. She circled the counter until she could face Melanie. "Oh, you didn't." The sinking feeling torpedoed her stomach. "Tell me you didn't go out with the fire breather."

A smile played on Melanie's lips. A fire breather. Joy should have seen him last night. The nickname would have really stuck. She continued rummaging around the shelves underneath, looking for the notebook. She hadn't been able to think clearly since Lance had left last night.

"I didn't go out with him, exactly. He was at the restaurant when we got there." Finding the book, she placed it on the counter and rose. "And he came to my rescue."

"Your rescue?" He didn't strike her like the kind of man who would bother rescuing a drowning kitten from a kiddy pool. "What was he rescuing you from?" Joy wanted to know.

Melanie thought of the way Bradley had looked at her when they'd first met.

"From what was shaping up to be one of the worst evenings of my life." She turned to go to the storeroom, but Joy caught her hand.

"Will you stand still and tell me the whole story?" she demanded with exasperation.

"Bradley was into planning the second year of my retirement, when I spotted Lance and pretended that he was my jealous boyfriend, out looking for me. I told Bradley that the last time he came looking for me, they never found the guy I was with. So Bradley did the only thing he could." She grinned, remembering. "He bolted and ran, leaving me to Lance's mercy."

"Something he doesn't look like he has a whole lot to spare." Joy took a deep breath, bracing herself. She wasn't sure if she was ready to hear this or not. But Melanie was her oldest, dearest friend, and she had an obligation to stick by her even when she was being reckless and crazy. "All right, fill me in. What did you do then?"

Melanie could almost see him standing there, a reluctant knight, ready to rescue and retreat. "I offered to buy him dinner to pay him back for rescuing me."

The offer didn't surprise Joy. Melanie was generous to a fault. What would surprise her, however, was learning that the fire breather was human enough to want to share an evening with a woman.

"And he let you?"

Melanie shook her head. Her so-called date probably would have, but not Lance. She had to admit, she was old-fashioned enough to like the gallantry Lance had exhibited. She smiled to herself. Lance would undoubtedly be annoyed at being called gallant. Too bad, she called them as she saw them.

"I thought he was, but when the waitress came with the bill, he paid for it. Insisted on it. And then he took me home."

"And then?"

Melanie couldn't help the sigh that escaped as she said, "And then he kissed me." She would probably sigh each time she remembered, for a long, long time. It wasn't the kind of kiss a woman took lightly, no matter how experienced she was.

Details, she wanted details, Joy thought, frustrated that she had to pull out every word. Melanie was usually a lot more talkative than this. If she'd given it any thought, she would have realized it was a bad sign.

"Where?"

Her eyes closed as she remembered. Melanie ran her tongue ever so lightly over her bottom lip. "On the mouth."

This was bad, Joy thought, studying Melanie's expression.

"No, I mean where were you when he kissed you? In the car, in the house?" She paused, afraid of the answer. "In the bedroom?"

If it had gone that far, Melanie would have refrained from sharing the fact with Joy. There was a time to take stock of loyalties and though she dearly loved Joy, Melanie knew that Lance wouldn't have appreciated her sharing all the intimate details of their time together.

Melanie put an end to Joy's speculation. "Don't open your eyes that wide, Joy. Your contact lenses are going to pop out. He kissed me at the front door, and he never came inside." She tried not to laugh at the disappointed

look on Joy's face. "I think he's afraid of a relationship."

"He's a man, isn't he?"

It wasn't like that with Lance, Melanie thought. "No,
there's more to it than that. I don't understand yet." A
look of determination came into her eyes. "But I intend
to."

The rumbling noise on the street in front of the shop
had her looking out the store window. A truck was pulling up. There were no deliveries scheduled for today.
The things from the last auction she'd attended weren't
due until the end of the week.

Melanie went to the front door and saw that the delivery truck belonged to a local florist. She looked over
her shoulder at Joy. "Is your husband in the doghouse
again?"

Joy joined her, her curiosity aroused. "If he is, I didn't
put him there."

The delivery man walked in a few minutes later, a
clipboard under his arm and a long, white box with the
florist's trademark in his hands. It was early, but he already looked harried. He singled out Melanie. "I've got
a delivery for a McCloud."

No one sent her flowers. The people she knew might
bring them to her personally, colorful things they'd
picked from their garden and arranged in a homemade
bouquet. No one thought to use a florist.

She wondered if it was a mistake. "That's me." She
eyed the box. "Who are they from?"

"It's on the card," he told her wearily. "Sign here,
please." He shoved the clipboard into her hand, tapping
the first space. When she finished, he traded her the box
for his clipboard. "Have-a-nice-day." The words

dripped from his mouth mechanically as he walked out again.

"Open it, open it," Joy urged. When Melanie didn't move quickly enough to satisfy her, Joy eased the other end off for her. "Oh, wow. Look at them."

"I am," Melanie murmured. Half a dozen long-stemmed yellow roses sat nestled in green tissue paper. They looked so beautiful, she almost didn't want to disturb them.

"Well, who's it from?" If they'd been for Joy, she would have torn into the envelope already. Didn't Melanie have *any* curiosity?

Melanie moved the tissue paper around, looking for a card.

"I haven't the vaguest idea." She removed one rose from the others and sniffed it. Pleasure embraced her. Whoever had sent them had asked for the scented kind to be delivered. She loved the smell of roses.

Joy took a guess. "Maybe it's Bradley, apologizing for running out on you last night. Maybe he wants another chance to get together." She looked at Melanie hopefully. According to Greg, Bradley's income was in the six-figure range. It would have been nice for Melanie if a little of that was spread around here. "If he talked to Greg, he knows you don't have a boyfriend."

This was one of those few times she didn't mind raining on Joy's parade. Not when she was the drum majorette. "If he knows that, then he knows I made the whole thing up. And, if he's as smart as he kept telling me he was, I think he's figured out *why* I made the whole thing up." Finding the card, she took it out and read it: "'I'm sorry I yelled at you last night. Lance.'" She tucked the note into her skirt pocket, curling her hand around it.

Joy's mouth dropped open. "He yelled at you?"

A small detail she hadn't mentioned. Melanie dismissed it now with a wave of her hand. "Things got a little emotional."

Joy looked at the roses again. Maybe this fire breather wasn't such a bad guy after all. "Obviously." She spread the paper back on either side of the box. The next move was Melanie's. She raised her eyes up to her friend. "So, what are you going to do?"

Melanie picked up the box and carried it to her office. "First, I'm going to put the roses in water, and then I'm goi:g to thank him for his flowers." Her eyes met Joy's. "In person."

"Sure you know what you're doing?"

Melanie set the box down on her desk. There was a vase around here somewhere, she thought. All she had to do was remember where. "I'm sure."

"That man isn't going to know what hit him."

"Yeah, he will." Melanie smiled at the photograph she had on her desk. Her aunt smiled back at her. Aunt Elaine, she knew, would have understood what was going on perfectly. "If I do it right."

Chapter Seven

She knew she was taking a chance hoping to find Lance in. Given the nature of his work, he could be out anywhere. The sensible thing would have been to call ahead. But if she did that, he would have made a point of not being around.

It made her smile to realize she was beginning to understand the way he operated.

So she took the chance. Maybe she'd be lucky.

The key to getting to someone like Lance, Melanie thought as she parked her car in the rear lot behind the fire station, was the element of surprise. That way, she might just be able to wiggle in and get close to him before he knew what was going on. Before the protective shields he kept around him had a chance to go down and lock into place.

At least it was worth a shot.

She tugged her hem down into place as she got out of the car and closed the door. The display did not go unnoticed. One of the firefighters broke away from the group gathered near the entrance and crossed over to her just as she walked in.

She recognized him as the man who'd given her Kelly's new address. Wide shouldered and about six foot four inches, Ed Thompson moved with more grace than she'd have thought possible for someone so big.

"Hi." He flashed her a wide grin. "Heard from Kelly yet?"

She found his smile infectious and wondered if he and Lance ever got together. Lance could stand a little of that easygoing manner rubbing off on him, she mused.

Melanie nodded in reply. "Just a few lines." She'd gotten the note yesterday, surprised that Kelly had responded so quickly. She'd sent him a parting gift. A vase used on the set of one of the MGM musicals in the fifties that he'd admired every time he'd come by the shop. "He's having a great time fishing. His wife isn't as thrilled as he is, but John figures she'll come around to his way of thinking."

Thompson laughed, the sound rich and deep. "Same old Kelly." He made an educated guess why she was here. "Looking for Reed?"

When she nodded, he could only marvel. The contrast between the two was like comparing the light and dark side of the moon. How did a guy like that merit a woman like her?

"Thought so. You're in luck. He's in. Popular guy this morning," he commented. "Well, if you'll excuse me, I've got some chili to make hot." Winking, he backed away, going down the long hallway to the station's kitchen.

Was Thompson just being cryptic or was there someone in Lance's office with him? She knew Lance wouldn't appreciate her popping in like this if he was talking to someone but it couldn't be helped. Besides, if he really didn't want to see her, he wouldn't have sent the roses. He would have just let it end without any further communication—other than maybe another citation, she thought.

Turning the corner, she made her way to his office. It was the last door before the rear exit. Perfect choice for him, she thought. It gave him the opportunity to come and go without being noticed.

There *was* someone in his office, Melanie realized, looking through the glass door. Sitting in front of his desk, the woman's back was to the door. Struck by the carefully styled, soft, gray hair, it took Melanie a moment to notice the cane leaning against the arm of her chair.

For the space of a heartbeat, Melanie debated quietly retreating. But she hadn't come this far, egging herself on, just to fade away without a word. Besides, the next time she might not be so lucky. The next time she came by, he might not be in.

Making up her mind, she rapped once. Without waiting for a response or an invitation that might not be forthcoming, she opened the door. "Hi, I don't mean to interrupt."

Lance looked up sharply at the sound of her voice. For a second he thought he was imagining her. The way he'd imagined her all through breakfast this morning, and all through his sleepless night the night before. She'd been preying on his mind ever since he'd kissed her. He cursed himself and her for it more than once in the past twelve hours.

It was only because he'd felt guilty about losing his cool and his control that his mind kept returning to her. That was the bill of goods he'd tried to sell himself, but as of yet, he still wasn't buying into the excuse a hundred percent. For that he needed time and distance. If having her show up here was any indication, she wasn't about to give him either.

Didn't mean to interrupt, he thought, silently mocking her apology. The hell she didn't. She enjoyed setting his world on its ear.

"Yeah, you did." The sigh that escaped his lips sounded almost resigned, and that worried him. "Otherwise you wouldn't have knocked. You would have turned around and gone home when you saw I was busy."

The woman in the chair had turned around as soon as Melanie spoke. Recognition on Melanie's part was instantaneous. It was the woman in the photograph on his desk.

Bess gave her nephew a fleeting frown. "Lance, that's no way to speak to a lady." The reprimand was tempered with humor. There was unabashed interest in the gray eyes as they swept over Melanie, taking measure of the young woman who seemed to be so familiar with Lance.

"That's all right," Melanie told her as, to Lance's mounting dismay, she walked in, "he sends roses when he's been rude." Her face seemed to bloom with pleasure as her eyes met his. "And I love roses."

The information that Lance had sent someone roses was immediately digested. There was no small show of mystification and delight on the round, genial face as Bess turned toward Lance.

"You sent her roses?"

Lance shifted uncomfortably. She was going to make a big deal out of this. "I—"

He got no further, not that he knew what he was going

to say if he had been allowed to speak. Other than the fact that sending roses to a woman shouldn't be a cause for rampant speculation as to motive and intent. What it was, was a mistake. He'd known it was a mistake the minute he'd hung up the phone after placing the order.

A moment of weakness was to blame. He'd done something wrong, and he'd wanted to make amends. Flowers were all he could think of. He knew how much Bess loved them. All women, he'd once been told, loved getting flowers. It seemed harmless enough at the time, and he *had* treated McCloud badly, and not just because he'd shouted into her face.

So he'd apologized by sending her flowers and inadvertently, he knew now, placed them on his own grave, as well.

Melanie felt the bond between her and Bess forming immediately. She warmed to her, almost from the moment she saw her. There was something in her eyes, in her smile, that reminded Melanie of Aunt Elaine.

"He did. The most beautiful yellow roses I've ever seen." Melanie raised her eyes to his face. "No one's ever sent me roses before."

Bess didn't bother hiding her surprise. "I find that difficult to believe. A lovely young lady like you?" She cast a side glance at her nephew. *Good for you,* she silently applauded.

Lance had no idea how to begin untangling the knot he watched forming in front of him.

If Melanie had learned nothing else during her unorthodox childhood, it was how to take a compliment graciously. She inclined her head. "Thank you, Aunt Bess. He obviously doesn't get his manners from you."

So, he'd talked about her to this woman, had he?

Bess's pleasure continued to increase. "You know who I am?"

In reply, Melanie crossed to Lance's desk and turned the photograph around for Bess to look at. "He showed me this the first time I was here."

Lance knew that pointing out that it was the *only* time she'd been here and that he hadn't shown her the photograph, she had taken it and asked, was only going to fall on deaf ears. For some reason he couldn't fathom, it pleased Bess to think that there was something going on between him and the energetic blonde.

One look at her eyes told him he was right. Bess looked as if she was barely suppressing her delight. "No wonder you haven't had time to stop by lately."

He had to set her straight now, before things became any more confused. "It's not like that, Bess," he protested with feeling. He groped for the right words. "She's just, just—"

"Very happy to meet you," Melanie concluded. Leaning over her, Melanie took Bess's hand and shook it. "I'm Melanie McCloud."

Bess and Elaine would have gotten on famously, Melanie thought. She could tell just by looking at the woman. She felt a pang, wishing her aunt could have met Bess.

"Lance tells me your favorite movie is *Next Year, Paris.*"

The amount of surprise ricocheting through Bess could have been measured on the Richter scale. Lance had always been closemouthed, even as a boy. She'd spent years worrying about him, about his finding someone who was up to the task of bringing out the man Bess knew in her heart still existed beneath the hard exterior the world saw.

Now it looked as if her prayers had been answered. If he'd told Melanie about her, about something so minute and trivial as her favorite movie, then he was finally opening up.

Casting a triumphant look in his direction, Bess said, "He told you that?"

Damn, this was getting worse and worse right in front of his eyes. He had to put a stop to it. Trying to get his aunt's attention away from Melanie, Lance leaned over his desk and put his hand on her arm.

"Bess, I—"

She waved his hand away. "Hush, Lance, I'm talking to Melanie if you don't mind. So, what else has my nephew told you?"

Making herself far more comfortable in his office than he had ever managed to, Melanie leaned a hip against the edge of his desk.

"Not very much." She leaned closer to Bess. "You know how he is."

Bess's eyes were soft, warm, as they washed over Lance quickly. A potpourri of memories crowded her head. She loved him dearly, but that didn't blind her to what he was. "Indeed I do."

And obviously, so did this young woman who had popped out of nowhere. Bess couldn't remember when she'd felt so pleased about something. There was a warmth about Melanie that had been conspicuously missing from Lauren. Bess had never felt easy about that match, but had said nothing because Lance had seemed so keen on her, and all Bess had ever wanted was his happiness.

When Lauren had walked out on Lance before he'd even been discharged from the hospital, Bess could have ripped the woman's heart out with her bare hands. But even if she'd been able to do that, there was nothing she could do to undo the damage Lauren had caused by her callous act.

But maybe there was something Melanie could do.

This one would stay no matter what, Bess thought, quietly regarding her. As long as Lance didn't do something awful to push her away.

Bess shifted her rather ample frame in the chair and looked at her nephew accusingly. "Lance, why didn't you tell me about Melanie?"

He threw up his hands in frustration. "Because there's nothing to tell."

To his mounting irritation, he saw his aunt and McCloud exchange knowing looks. McCloud shrugged carelessly. The gesture fairly shouted "You know how men are." He should never have sent those damn flowers.

"Is there any reason you're here now?" he demanded impatiently.

Her smile was a direct contrast to the expression on his face. "I just came by to thank you for the roses. They arrived this morning just as I opened up the shop."

Bess latched on to this newest piece of information like a magnet sweeping over scattered iron filings. "You have a shop?"

Melanie nodded proudly. "It's on Main and Thiel. I sell memorabilia. Props and costumes from old movies, autographs from celebrities, posters, lobby cards. Things like that."

It was tantamount to telling a child that she worked at the North Pole as first assistant to Santa Claus. Bess's eyes grew almost as round as Joy's had this morning. "Really?"

Lance rose to his feet. Enough was enough. He

couldn't continue to just sit here and listen to this any-more. God only knew where the momentum was going to take the two of them. And him. Besides he needed to take an early lunch today.

"C'mon, Bess, I don't have that long for lunch, and I've got a couple of appointments scheduled for this af-ternoon." Putting Kelly's work on hold, Lance was turn-ing his attention back to his own thick file of work. The warehouse fire was looking more and more like the work of an arsonist. He had more important things to worry about than a blonde who kept popping up in his life at inopportune moments.

Lance rounded the desk and took his aunt's arm, care-fully helping her to her feet. He fully intended to put Melanie behind him, both physically and mentally. Just as soon as he aired out the office and got rid of that damned scent she wore.

Bess leaned on Lance's arm, but her eyes were on Melanie. And her mind was busy making plans. "Would you like to join us for lunch?"

Oh, no, he wasn't about to break bread with Melanie twice. Once had had disastrous effects. "I'm sure she has other things to do, Bess."

The smile on Melanie's lips dashed his hopes of a clean escape. "No, I don't."

"There, you see?" Bess declared triumphantly. She had a good feeling about this, she thought, looking at Melanie. A very good feeling.

Didn't she have work to do? Some place to be? "What about your shop?" Lance reminded her.

If he meant to chase her away, he was going to have to do better than that, Melanie thought, falling into step beside Bess.

"It's slow today," she told him. "Joy can handle it for a while."

Joy might be able to handle whatever went on at the shop, but Lance had a feeling that he wouldn't be able to handle what was happening here. Not when there were two women ganging up on him. Especially since one of the women was Bess.

He gave it one last try. "Bess, the reservations are for two."

Bess had no idea why he was being so stubborn about resisting this. Melanie seemed absolutely perfect to her. "There's always room for one more. We're not going to a fancy restaurant, for heaven's sake. We don't need reservations. Don't be rude, Lance," she chided with a bit more feeling.

Her eyes bright with interest, Bess asked, "So, tell me how you and Lance met."

"I wrote her up for several fire code violations," he growled, hoping that put an end to any romantic misconceptions Bess was entertaining, although something told him he should have known better.

Bess looked over her shoulder at her nephew. "Yes, that sounds just like you."

Rather than let Lance lead her out of the fire station, Bess hooked her arm through Melanie's, leaning heavily on her cane with her other hand. "So, Melanie, tell me more about this shop of yours...."

The best thing about having Melanie come to lunch with them was that he didn't have to talk much.

Lance judged that he didn't have to talk at all if he didn't want to. The upside of that was that he didn't have to politely fend off Bess's questions about what he was doing with his private life and the direction his life *wasn't* going in.

Not having to talk also meant he was spared making up excuses about why he hadn't gotten together with his father yet. And why he hadn't managed to get himself to forgive him. It was a cause Bess championed even more heartily than trying to match him up with someone.

More like a crusade, really, he amended silently as he sat back and listened to Melanie charm the ruffles right off his aunt. But how was he supposed to forgive and forget fifteen years of neglect? Fifteen years of being without a father? Fifteen years of thinking that somehow, deep down, it was all his fault?

The simple answer was that he couldn't. There was no point in even trying.

He looked at Bess. She'd taken him in when his father had gone off to lick his wounds and grieve, taken him in and never once thrown it up into his face that her life had become harder because there was someone to look after now. Someone who made demands on her time and space, however unintentionally and silently. Someone who gave her grief just because he couldn't find any peace within himself and took it out on the world at large.

Bess had always looked after him, not that he gave her an easy time of it. There was a point during his teen years when it looked as if he'd wind up spending his adult life on the wrong side of prison bars if he continued on the path he was on.

It was Bess who had literally knocked sense into his head, boxing his ears with those small fists of hers. It was when he saw just how much she cared, how important he was to her and how much he'd hurt her because of the self-destructive path he was on that he'd taken stock of himself and finally straightened out.

So, if she made him a little crazy with her requests and her nudging him along to make peace with his father, he forgave her. She meant well. All the questions and minilectures were all couched in love.

He owed Bess a lot. A great deal more than he did the man who had given him life and walked out of it years later.

Lance had no idea what he owed Melanie.

His immediate response would have been "nothing," but something nagged at him, refusing to allow him to let it go at just that. He didn't know if it was the way she looked at him or the way she'd felt, her compact, firm body pressed tightly against his when he'd kissed her. Or maybe it was because when he was around her, he could almost believe that good things were possible.

Almost.

He wondered what made a woman like her tick. Where did she see all the good that she saw?

And why wouldn't she just leave him alone?

What did she want with him, anyway? He'd given her no reason to believe that there was anything between them, or that there ever could be.

Yeah, right. Nothing except a kiss that had singed both of them and half a dozen yellow roses to prove what an insensitive guy he was.

What the hell was he doing, anyway?

He looked at the cola he was having and wished it was a scotch and soda instead. A double. Then maybe the questions rattling around in his head wouldn't matter.

And maybe then he could stop smelling her damn perfume across the table.

The two women were getting on fabulously. He'd

never seen his aunt so taken with anyone. He had to admit that McCloud seemed to have that effect on people, drawing them out into the light.

Like him.

Since his input wasn't sought, he would have liked to have tuned the conversation going on around him completely out. But, like a man standing at his own execution, waiting for the ax to fall, he couldn't tear his attention away.

And eventually, it happened. The ax fell. With a resounding thud.

"So then it's settled." Bess placed her hand over Melanie's and smiled broadly. "You'll come."

Come? Come where? Lance looked uneasily from one woman to the other. It figured. The second he'd allowed himself to drift off, he missed a crucial piece of conversation.

"Come to what?" he asked suspiciously.

"Trust a man not to listen." Bess shook her head. "To my birthday party. You probably forgot."

There was no censure in the chide. Bess knew Lance had a great deal on his mind. But she had her own reasons for having a party this year. A reason that went beyond just wanting those she held dear around her.

"I know it might be foolish, throwing my own birthday party," she confided to Melanie, "but at my age, well, I don't really care about how things look anymore."

"There's nothing wrong with throwing your own birthday party," Melanie insisted. "I think it's a great idea. Who knows better what you want at your own party than you?"

"I do like this girl, Lance," Bess enthused. That,

Lance thought, was abundantly clear. "And you'll come?" she asked again.

Melanie stole a look at Lance. It was obvious that he was far from happy about the invitation. He looked as though he would like nothing better than to have her just disappear.

She wasn't about to disappear. "I would love to come, Bess."

"Won't you be busy?" Lance looked at Melanie pointedly, hoping she would pick up the hint.

The look on her face was pure, unfiltered innocence. Her blue eyes delved straight into his soul, unsettling him more than he wanted to think about.

"No."

A strange sort of desperation clawed at him. He didn't want her slipping so effortlessly, so seamlessly into his life. He didn't want her there. Because if she was, he might start to get used to it, start to even expect it. And that would be the worst thing of all.

He tried again. "I thought you were holding a big tea party or something."

He'd only partially read the flyer that was up on her show window, Melanie thought, surprised that he had noticed at all.

"No, that's on the following Saturday." She saw the curiosity in Bess's eyes and quickly explained. "We're celebrating the fiftieth anniversary of the release of *The Thief Of Hearts*." She smiled at Lance. "After, of course, I make sure that the store is fire safe." Her eyes shifted to Bess. "Would you like to attend? I even have the jacket and vest Stewart O'Donnell wore in the hunting scene." How she'd come by it was a story she was looking forward to sharing with Bess at leisure.

"My dear, I would love to attend," Bess declared, one eye on Lance.

He felt as if someone had just slammed the door to his prison cell. The sound even echoed in his head.

"What did you think you were doing?" Lance demanded after he'd made certain Bess was on her way home.

"Could you narrow that down a bit for me?" Melanie requested. "Do you mean at the restaurant, or on the way back, or—"

He gritted his teeth. No one was that thick. "I mean from the minute you walked into my office."

"Being polite to your aunt?" Melanie guessed at the answer he was looking for. "And it's not hard at all, she's a doll."

"Yes, she is," he agreed with her, "and I don't want that 'doll' thinking that there's something going on between us."

Large, cornflower blue eyes looked up into his. "And there isn't."

She was mocking him, he thought, fighting the urge to tell her what he thought of her little act. Fighting even harder to keep from taking her into his arms and kissing that confident, impudent smile right off her face.

"No."

She touched his face so lightly, it was as if it had been brushed by the wings of a butterfly. A smile played on her lips and in her eyes. "Liar."

He'd had just about all he could take. "McCloud—"

She heard the warning note in his voice and ignored it. "Sorry, my lunch hour is over. I have to go and rescue Joy."

And who, he wondered, banking down a feeling that wasn't altogether that unpleasant if he stopped to analyze it, was going to rescue him?

Chapter Eight

"Hey, wait up."

Melanie stopped and turned around, half hoping that it was Lance calling out to her. But the voice was too deep to belong to him.

And it didn't. A firefighter she'd been introduced to by John Kelly named Able McCarthy was hurrying toward her.

He gave Lance a cursory nod before turning to Melanie. There was a pleased look on his ruddy face. "I talked to Kelly last night. He said he just got that vase you sent to him. Told me he thought you were being way too generous."

The vase had been a prop in a pivotal scene of a musical. Its only real value was sentimental. Melanie grinned. "He always admired it whenever he came into my shop. He said that someday he wanted to buy it for his wife." She knew he was still raising his grandson and that times were tight for the older man and his wife.

"Tell him when you speak to him that I thought it was time 'someday' came along for him."

"I'll be sure to tell him that." With the air of someone who suddenly realized that he might be interrupting something, Able looked from Melanie to Lance, who had stopped to listen to the conversation, and then mumbled that he had to get back to work.

So, he wasn't the only one she gave things to, Lance thought. Just how did she plan on staying in business? "You keep giving your stock away like that, you're not going to make any money."

It wasn't hard to guess what he thought of her business acumen. Melanie shrugged carelessly. She was far more interested in the delight Kelly had expressed when he'd received her gift. "I'm not in it for the money."

It was an entirely altruistic statement, and he didn't believe her for a minute. Everyone was always in it for the money. "Oh, then what are you in it for?"

She heard the cynicism in his voice, and it bothered her, both because he obviously thought she was lying and because he couldn't believe that there were people motivated by something other than cash flow and the accumulation of wealth.

Melanie lifted her chin, daring him to dispute her. "The pleasure."

For perhaps a minute he could almost believe her. The light in her eyes had told him that was exactly what she was feeling when McCarthy relayed Kelly's message. Either she possessed the world's most generous heart— or she was just a fool. In either case, he would've hated to have been her accountant.

Lance hooked his thumbs on his belt loops, his eyes on hers. "Can't bank pleasure."

She begged to differ with that. It was all in the way

you interpreted your ultimate gain. "Yes, you can. And, just like money in the bank, it grows."

He had little to no patience with people who weren't logical or practical. "You're even crazier than I thought."

The remark stung and she almost retreated. She really did have to be getting back. But something kept her rooted to where she stood, making her unable, and unwilling, to tear herself away. A strange yet familiar feeling wafted through her. She concentrated on it until she could grasp it and understand why it was nagging at her this way.

And then she remembered. "You know, I had a dog once."

Lance groaned. This was what he got for lingering. He should have just let her get into her car and leave, without bothering to see her off.

"Is this going to be a 'Lassie Come Home' story, because if it is, I have to warn you that my lunch is liable to come up."

She ignored the image and the sentiment behind it. "No, this is going to be a 'Lassie Didn't Want A Home' story." Melanie looked at him pointedly. "Or, at least, that was the way 'Lassie' behaved. Actually, it was a male dog and I called him Petey."

The wind was teasing the ends of her hair around, blowing it toward him. He stepped back and tried to tell himself that he was completely unaffected by it and by the scent the breeze insisted on sending his way. Her scent. Vanilla and wildflowers. And something more.

"Fascinating."

Melanie ignored the sarcasm. "Petey was a mongrel. He wandered into our backyard one day and snarled and barked at everyone who came near him."

"My kind of dog," he quipped. "Why didn't you have animal services come and get him?"

"When you see the wizard, be sure to ask him for a heart." She shook her head. The answer should have been obvious. "Because if animal services took him to the pound, no one was ever going to adopt him. After a while, they would have had to put him to sleep. Nobody wants a snarling dog."

Except for her, he thought. McCloud would have wanted him. Probably too blind and too stubborn to realize the deck was stacked against her. "So you set out to tame him."

Her eyes held his. "Not to tame him, just to give him what he needed."

Lance tried to ignore the parallel that was staring him in the face. Or, at the very least, take offense. "Food," he guessed.

"That," Melanie conceded, "and love. He needed that more." *Just like you do, Lance. You need someone to care, to love you.* "Someone had really done a number on him and it took Petey a long time to trust anyone." As she spoke, her mouth curved fondly. "But he did. Finally. After that, he was like a completely different dog."

Lance didn't care for analogies, and he hated being preached to. That was Bess's prerogative, and he only let her exercise it on occasion. McCloud had no business preaching to him. She hadn't earned the right.

"So, what is this, some hidden message here? You're telling me that you think I'm a dog?" His brows drew together in a dark line as he dared her to get out of this gracefully.

"No, but there are some very striking similarities here." Unable to stop herself, she touched his cheek, lightly skimming it with her fingers. He didn't draw away immediately. "I think you need a little kindness, Lance. More than that, to *believe* in a little kindness." Her eyes begged him to listen. And to hear. "Let someone be kind to you, Lance. It's all right if you do," she said softly.

What was she trying to do to him? Make him believe in what she was saying only to get cut down again? To be left completely defenseless again? He'd already been there, and he had no intention of going there again, of living through it again.

"No, it's not."

She read between the lines. "What are you afraid of?"

He didn't know what possessed him to be honest. Maybe it was the sound of her voice, lulling his senses for the briefest of moments. Maybe, when all else failed, the truth would work. And make her back away.

"Of liking you too much."

"Too much," Melanie repeated, savoring the taste of the words on her tongue. The smile, soft and gentle, began in her eyes and filtered all through her before it worked its power on him and drew him in as well. "Does that mean you already like me a little?"

Yeah, he did, and he deserved to have his head examined for signs of mental deterioration. "What, are you switching from 'Lassie' to 'Columbo' now?"

She smiled up into his eyes until he found himself smiling too. Just a little. "Whatever it takes."

Lance echoed the phrase like some dazed teenager, mesmerized by the light in her eyes. "Whatever it takes for what?"

She'd never believed in playing games, in being coy or hard to get. She wanted this man, and if the game was too hard, he wouldn't stick around to play. She knew that without being told. So she loaded the dice and threw them, hoping for luck.

"To get you to kiss me again."

All through lunch, watching her talk to his aunt, watching her lips move, he'd thought about nothing but making them move against his.

He felt like some damned idiot under a damned hypnotic spell.

Lance had no strength to even pretend to protest. "Hell, why didn't you say so?"

She stood perfectly still before him, her face turned up to his. "You don't react well to direct requests."

"Neither do you." The front of the station was deserted. He blocked everything else out of his mind. Except for the mouth that looked like ripe berries and honey. "Shut up, McCloud."

She saw McCarthy peering out beside the main fire engine. Lance wasn't the type who liked being observed. "But—"

"See what I mean?" Didn't the woman ever stop talking? How could he kiss her if her lips kept forming words? "Shut up, McCloud," he repeated, combing his fingers through her hair. "So I can kiss you."

Melanie did as she was told, sinking into the sensation that she'd been recreating in her mind ever since his lips had first touched hers. She could feel the pulse in her throat throbbing wildly, like the mad flutter of a hummingbird's wings as it tried to remain in place. Lance deepened the kiss.

It was just like before.

No, better. It was better than before.

A woman could get easily addicted to this, she thought, winding her arms around his neck.

He had to stop doing this, Lance thought.

Okay, in a minute. In just a minute he was going to stop doing this. He was going to stop fouling himself up and walk away from her. Really.

He was going to stop.

Just as soon as he tasted a little more of her lips, drank a little more from the well she seemed so intent on dragging him to, then he'd stop.

Cold turkey, he'd stop.

Just one second more.

Lance wrapped his arms more tightly around her, completely unaware of how his hands had come to be there. Last he remembered, his fingers had been in her hair.

And his mind had been lost from the start.

"Hey, Reed, get a room!" The hooted mandate echoed in his ears.

Reluctantly, Lance drew away from her. But not completely. Cold turkey was not what it was cracked up to be.

His heart still beating fast, he looked at her incredulously. "What is it about you that makes me forget things?"

She drew air greedily into her lungs. She'd completely forgotten to breathe. She'd forgotten everything except how much she loved the feel of his mouth on hers.

"Must be the taste of the lipstick I wear." Dynamite, she thought, she was playing with dynamite. She knew what happened to people who played with dynamite. They wound up being blown to smithereens.

Maybe, she mused, she already had been.

"So," she let out a breath that was decidedly shaky. "I'll see you."

Anything to make her leave now, before he embarrassed himself even further. "Yeah."

Just at her car door, she turned to look at him. "At the party?"

He nodded, knowing he shouldn't let her come. Knowing it was futile to tell her not to. The worst of it was that he wanted her there. So he could see her again without asking to.

"I don't know where Bess lives," she suddenly realized.

It was his opportunity to be flippant and turn on his heel, cutting the tie. He didn't do it, which just proved to him that he was a bigger damn fool than he thought. "I'll pick you up."

Melanie smiled.

"Nice little piece of work, isn't she?" Able commented. He came out from around the fire truck just as Melanie pulled away. He saw the warning look come into Lance's eyes and decided to go ahead, anyway. "I guess I was wrong about you."

Lance raised a brow that cautioned the other man to weigh his words. "Meaning?"

"The guys and I thought you were a cold bastard." Able laughed. The deep, rumbling sound saved him from a scathing comment. "I guess you're not so cold after all. Couldn't be if Melanie's interested in you."

Lance looked at the other man sharply. "You know her?"

"Been to her shop a couple of times. Kelly took me," he explained, in case Lance attached a certain meaning to a man browsing through the kind of things she had on display. "My wife likes that sort of stuff," he added before he admitted, "kinda found it interesting myself. Wouldn't want to see someone like her hurt."

Able looked a little too broad to make it as a guardian angel. He was more suited to being someone's idea of The Hulk. In any case, Lance didn't like being warned. "She's old enough to take care of herself, don't you think?"

Able's wide shoulders rose in a half shrug. "A woman like Melanie makes a guy feel protective."

It was on the tip of Lance's tongue to tell Able what he, and any of the others who felt compelled to tell him how to behave, could do with their warnings. But then he let it go. Why pick a fight over something he didn't intend to do, anyway? He didn't intend to get close enough to Melanie to necessitate being warned away.

All he had to do, he thought, was maintain a safe distance from her.

Like in another country.

Had there been a rug in front of the window, Melanie was sure she would have worn a path in it by now. As it was, she was going to have to buff that section of the floor if it was going to match the rest. She'd been crossing to the window every few minutes to watch for Lance for almost an hour.

Admittedly she had begun early, but she couldn't help herself. She was always ready early.

And Lance arrived late.

Relief and pleasure flowing through her, Melanie was opening the door for him before he had a chance to press the bell.

He looked at her in surprise, his hand poised to ring. What, did she intuit doorbells now, too?

She stepped back only to reach for her purse. "I was beginning to think you weren't going to come."

"I considered it."

Well, at least he was being honest with her. That was something. She pulled the door closed behind her. The soft "click" told her it was secured. One hand wrapped around the gift she'd selected for Bess, she threaded her other hand through his arm.

Her fingers wound around the hard muscles. "But you came."

"Yeah, I came." He opened the passenger door for her, knowing it wasn't considered politically correct these days and not giving a damn. He waited for her to get in, then closed the door. "I decided that bringing you with me was easier than listening to Bess lecture me all evening."

She laughed. Certainly couldn't accuse him of turning her head with his silver tongue. "Anyone ever suggest you get a job with the welcoming committee? You seem to have a certain natural flare for it."

He wasn't in the mood to be teased. He'd just struggled long and hard with himself over this, over something that shouldn't have even come up as far as he was concerned.

"This can't go anywhere." Muttering under his breath, Lance rounded the hood.

Melanie waited until he got in before looking at him innocently. "You mean there's something wrong with the car?"

He was sure she knew what he meant. But he wanted to go on record so everything was perfectly clear to her. Then, no matter what happened, she wouldn't be on his damn conscience. "No, I meant that this...this 'thing' between us." He jabbed his key into the ignition. "It can't go anywhere."

Melanie picked up on something he hadn't realized

he'd let slip. "Oh, so now you're willing to admit that there *is* something between us."

He drove the car into traffic and turned on the radio. He needed something to compete with the noise she was making.

"I'm not admitting anything," he said stubbornly. He caught the glance she gave him and mentally threw up his hands. "All right, yes, I'm admitting there's something there. What, I don't know, but I do know what it can't be."

She waited for him to tell her. When he didn't, she pressed, "And that is—"

"Permanent."

Had she given him the impression that she wanted to bag him and run off to the nearest all-night chapel? He very obviously needed to have a few things set straight.

"You're taking some giant leaps here, Lance, but for now, I'll leap with you. Just for the sake of argument, mind you, why can't it be permanent?" she asked gamely.

He thought of the old woman. Of his father. And his mother. Lauren wasn't even part of the equation anymore. "Because nothing is."

Because he was facing the road, she couldn't read his eyes. "Are we speaking metaphorically or from experience?"

Since when had they become a "we"? "Both," he said with exasperation.

Everything pointed to a woman, she figured. A woman who'd left scars. "Who left you, Lance?"

He wove around a truck and waited until they came to a stop at a red light before answering. "You want the whole list or the condensed version?"

He wasn't going to scare her off with that Big Bad

Wolf routine of his. She could be just as stubborn as he was. "The unabridged one."

He wasn't about to tell her about Lauren. A man had his pride. "Nobody."

She watched the muscle in his cheek tighten. "I don't believe you."

He didn't care if she did or not. He wasn't admitting to anything. "That isn't my problem."

"No, it's not. Your problem is that you don't trust anyone, even yourself."

That sounded like a lot of psychobabble. She hadn't struck him as someone who went in for that sort of thing. "Me?"

"You don't trust your feelings. You think that if you let them get out of the neat little cage you've shoved them into, something bad is going to happen."

"It is." He stared straight ahead, even though they were at a red light. "I'm going to care."

She laid her hand on his. How could there be such comfort in such a small gesture? He tried to detach himself from it, from her.

"And that's bad?"

"Only if you don't mind having your teeth kicked down your throat." That's how he'd felt watching Lauren walk away from him—as if his teeth had all been knocked down his throat. He hadn't been able to talk or make a sound. All he could do that entire night was just listen to himself breathe and wonder why he still did.

It had been really bad for him, she thought, moved. But she knew that the last thing he wanted from her was pity. "I've never kicked anyone's teeth down their throat, Lance. It's much too messy."

He curbed the desire to laugh. "That's what you say now."

Melanie shook her head. He was pulling up in front of a Victorian house complete with a white verandah that looked almost eerie in the moonlight. Perched on an incline, it was the last house on the block. Melanie was struck by its grace and poise. Like its owner, she mused.

"That's what I say always." Her eyes begged for a smile as they teased him. "I have references to that effect."

"Former lovers?" And why that should bother him so much when he didn't care was completely beyond him.

"No...present friends," she countered.

He was beginning to believe that maybe that was a very large club. So why was it so important to her to have him included in it?

The laugh was short and without humor. "Yeah, I think one of them warned me the other day about being nice to you. McCarthy," he said in reply to the question he saw in her eyes. "You got yourself some network there, lady."

"And there're no annual dues to join." *Laugh, Lance, I'm only teasing you.*

"What do you want with me, McCloud? You've obviously got so many other friends hanging around."

"Always room for more." Her voice lost its teasing note. "And, like I already told you, I think you need a friend."

He didn't need a friend. He didn't need anything, except to be left alone. That included by her. *Especially* by her, he thought.

Lance pulled up the emergency brake and switched off his lights. "And you're volunteering."

Melanie nodded. He wasn't about to scare her off with

ridicule. She'd endured worse for less. "Waving my hand so hard it's making a breeze."

The seat belt snapped back as he pressed the release. Lance turned in his seat to look at her. The gifts, the philosophy, the way she seemed to want to give of herself and mean it—it all baffled him. *She* baffled him.

"I don't know what to make of you, McCloud. I'm not sure if I've ever met anyone like you."

She didn't want to be unraveled. That would just be wasting time. "Don't make anything of me. Just take me as I am, Lance."

"What—" his mouth quirked "—a pain in the neck?"

Melanie refused to take offense. "Hey, it's a beginning."

He laughed then, and it felt good to laugh. Almost as good to laugh again as it did to kiss her. "You really are one of a kind, McCloud."

She never thought of herself as being unique in any way. "I am if you want me to be."

He knew what she was saying—that she wasn't different from everyone else. And that everyone else was a lot nicer than he was allowing himself to believe. But she was wrong. He'd seen the world for what it was, and it wasn't all pink roses the way she painted it.

Or all yellow roses, either.

But there was something irresistible about her. Something that kept drawing him in. Like a fish stuck on a hook. "You're going to regret getting mixed up with me, McCloud."

He sounded as if he was giving her a guarantee. But she had a feeling, a very strong feeling, that he was wrong. "I never regretted taking Petey in."

Maybe a little of her story had gotten to him. "Where's the mutt now?"

"Gone."

That, he thought, just underscored his point. "Finally ran away?"

She shook her head. There was an ache in her heart as she told him. "No, he died in my arms. He was pretty old by then. Old and tired. But he died warm and loved."

He saw the tears in her eyes and couldn't help marveling at the compassion she seemed to have for everyone and everything.

If he loved someone—if he could have loved someone, Lance amended, it would have been her.

But he couldn't, so it was all a moot point.

Chapter Nine

She blended in.

Leaning against the wall, sipping a beer that wasn't really cold enough, Lance watched Melanie in quiet awe. She appeared to be talking to several people at the same time. From where he stood, she didn't miss a beat. It hardly surprised him.

Melanie seemed to blend in with people as well as he didn't. It didn't seem to matter to her that, up until a couple of hours ago, she didn't know anyone gathered here at Bess's house except for Bess and him. Anyone walking into his aunt's house right now would have sworn that Melanie had known these people all her life. She certainly acted that way. And they all responded in kind, warming to her instantly.

Lance took another long pull from the dark amber bottle. No, it wasn't his imagination. The beer was much too warm. He was going to have to take a look at Bess's refrigerator. The temperature gauge was probably off again.

Melanie's laughter floated to him above the conversation.

His eyes found hers, and he lifted his bottle in a silent salute. He realized that he was smiling. Maybe she was finally working a little of her magic on him, as well.

He'd been that happy once, Lance thought, still watching her. Oh, not to the point where he could make people feel as if he was friendship in a box, wrapped up with a bright ribbon the way McCloud could, but he'd been happy. For him. There was a time when he'd actually enjoyed having conversations with people, instead of just wishing they'd go away and leave him the hell alone.

And then his mother had died and his father had left. Things had just fallen apart from there.

Lance set the bottle down on a side table. He had a bad taste in his mouth.

And just when things looked as if they were finally pulling themselves together, just when he'd found what he wanted to do with his life, found the woman he wanted to spend his life with, everything had exploded. Leaving him with shreds of a life. Teaching him that the only stable thing was emptiness.

His eyes shifted back to Melanie. She was trying to ease herself out of the circle that had gathered around her. Away from them and toward him.

What the hell was he doing, standing here in his aunt's living room, watching her? Wanting her. Wondering what it would be like to be with her. Maybe even for more than just a little while...

He should have his head examined.

"I'm glad you brought her."

Lance felt Bess's hand on his shoulder. The hand that had so often tried to soothe away his boyhood problems.

She deserved better than him for a nephew, he thought ruefully.

And Melanie deserved a man who could make her happy. And that wasn't him.

He reached for the bottle again. Might as well not let it go to waste, he thought philosophically, wishing for something stronger. He knew better than to ask. To Bess beer *was* hard liquor.

"Didn't have much choice," he told her, still watching Melanie. She hadn't made all that much progress in extricating herself. Served her right for being so damn cheerful all the time. People wanted cheer in their lives, even if they had to borrow it. *Most* people, he amended, but not him. "She would have hunted me down if I didn't."

Bess laughed. He could make up all the excuses he wanted to, but she wasn't about to be taken in by any of them.

"You always have a choice, Lance. I'm glad you made the right one for a change."

"Yeah, well…" He shrugged, letting the rest of the sentence fade away. He didn't want to get into it right now.

In her own subtle way, Bess had been after him for quite some time to find "a good woman," as she liked to put it, and settle down. As if there was some game preserve somewhere that stocked women like that. She just couldn't make her peace with the fact that he was going to remain unattached. He'd had different thoughts once, but that just wasn't supposed to happen for him.

He nodded toward the kitchen where he had glimpsed a very pretty, very large cake. "Isn't it about time you try to blow out the candles on that cake of yours?" He leaned over and whispered, "I've got the station on alert."

Bess swatted him away from her ear and heard him laugh. Bess glanced at her watch, then at the door.

"Not yet." Her eyes shifted toward him accusingly. "And I'll have you know, you impudent young pup, I'm not that old."

Impulsively, because she was the only one he still willingly allowed into his heart, Lance brushed her cheek with a kiss.

"You're right. You're probably a lot younger than I am, Bess. You just need a young man to bring it out, that's all." He saw the look she gave him and met it with an innocent one as he raised one hand in a gesture of surrender. "Never said a word."

He was behaving like the old Lance, Bess thought. The boy she remembered. She silently blessed the woman he'd brought with him. It was because of her; there was absolutely no doubt in Bess's mind. She'd seen the two of them together, and though Lance tried to remain distant, the distance wasn't quite as pronounced as before.

He just needed to come around a little more, that was all.

She turned to him abruptly. "Get some more cider and soda cans out of the spare refrigerator for me, will you, Lance?" She pointed to the table that she'd stocked before guests had begun arriving. "We seem to be running out."

Having dispatched him to the garage, Bess beckoned for Melanie and waited until she reached her.

Bess shifted her position until she could slip her free hand around Melanie's shoulders. "I sent Lance on a quick errand. I wanted to get you alone for a second so I could tell you how grateful I am to you.''

Melanie flushed with pleasure. She knew Bess would like the scarf she'd selected. It had once belonged to Greer Garson. The two women had similar coloring. But she regretted having missed out on seeing Bess's face when she'd unwrapped the present.

''You opened my gift already?''

It took her a second to realize what Melanie was saying. Bess laughed. ''Not the one with the pretty paper around it.'' Her gift was still on the side table, sitting jauntily atop the others where everyone could see its unique wrapping paper. Caricatures of movie stars from the thirties and forties vied for space on the robin's egg blue paper. ''The bigger one.'' She nodded toward the garage. ''Lance.''

Melanie slowly shook her head. ''I'm not quite sure I follow you.''

Bess smiled at the display of modesty. The girl would never take credit for it. It wasn't in her nature. ''You don't have to follow me. Just promise me that you'll stay around.''

Bess's eyes held Melanie's. The party and the people, all people she cared about, temporarily faded into the background. There were two people whom Bess loved dearly in this world, and one of them was out in the garage, rummaging for cider. Just like he was rummaging to find his way in life. Melanie could help him find it. Bess was sure of it.

''I don't know how things are between the two of you,'' she began slowly. ''Knowing Lance the way I do, you probably don't, either. But I want you to know that you're making a difference in his life. He won't say it, but I can see it in his eyes.'' She regarded the younger woman fondly. Melanie was exactly the kind of woman she'd envisioned for Lance. "You're bringing the light back to them. To him."

"I think you're giving me way too much credit."

"I don't." Remembering, her expression darkened. "After Lauren left, he was as black as the ashes of the fire they pulled him out of."

"Lauren?" Lance hadn't talked about anyone named Lauren. "The woman he tried to save from the burning building?" she guessed.

"No, the woman he was engaged to." Bess's eyes narrowed as she remembered the all-consuming hurt she'd witnessed in his eyes. She'd feared then that he wouldn't pull through. Wouldn't want to. And when Bruce had flown to his son's bedside from Seattle, to try one last time to patch things up between them, Lance had gotten even worse. Withdrawing so far away Bess thought no one and nothing would ever reach him again. "The woman who took one look at his burned, bandaged body in the hospital, believed the worst when the doctors told her that there was a strong chance he wouldn't walk again and fled. I guess she was afraid she'd actually have to do something substantial, like be there for him when he needed her."

Bess shrugged. It was over with and best left where it belonged. In the past. "I saw her leaving as a blessing in disguise. Lauren was very shallow." Pausing, she gave Lance's ex-fiancée her due. "Very pretty, but very shallow. The kind whose loyalty would be found wanting anytime it was tested." Bess looked at Melanie for a long moment. "Not like you."

It warmed her to be thought so well of, but the pedestal Bess was placing her on was a high perch from which to fall. "I'm flattered, Bess, but you don't know me."

"I'm sixty-seven today. I've been around a long time. I've learned a lot of things." Her eyes crinkled with laugh lines as she smiled. "Especially how to read people."

It was futile to argue with her and Melanie knew it. Bess was a lot like Elaine. Set in her ways and accustomed to being proven right.

Bess looked toward the garage and sighed impatiently. Lance was probably using the errand as an excuse to stay away from the party for as long as he could.

"Now, why don't you go see what's keeping that nephew of mine? I sent him into the garage to get a few extra bottles of cider and a few cans of soda." She pointed toward the door that led into the garage. "He seems to have gotten lost."

"Consider him retrieved," Melanie said, going after him.

"I consider him saved," Bess said under her breath before she turned toward one of her guests.

Melanie heard the voices before she even opened the door leading into the garage. Polite, strained voices with enough combustible tension behind them to set off a warehouse full of firecrackers.

Stepping into the garage, she saw that the outer door was open. A silver BMW was parked behind Bess's sedan, its tail just barely shy of the street. There was a man standing beside it.

A well-dressed man wearing a three-piece, dark suit, who, she thought as she went forward, looked a great deal like Lance. It was as if someone had taken Lance's photograph and used a computer-enhanced program to age it approximately ten years or so.

Both men stopped talking and turned toward her in unison. Melanie inclined her head toward the other man in a silent greeting, trying very hard not to stare. Lance hadn't told her he had an older brother. But then, Lance hadn't told her a great many things.

Slipping her arm around his waist in a gesture that Lance found far too familiar and comfortable for his own good, she looked up at him and said, "Bess is wondering where you are."

The words were directed toward Lance, but it was the other man who offered an excuse. "I was delayed. Traffic."

Melanie could feel Lance's whole body become rigid. "At least you thought to show up," Lance ground out tersely.

There was no anger in the other man's face at the veiled accusation. If anything, he looked resigned. Melanie couldn't help wondering if she'd stumbled onto a family feud of some sort.

"It's Bess's birthday," he pointed out. "I wouldn't have missed that."

Lance's face was impassive. Hard. As if birthdays meant nothing to him. "I can think of others you've missed."

"Lance, I—" the man began and stopped.

The argument that was brewing would leave the confines of politeness at any second, Melanie sensed, escalating into something ugly. Things were going to be said that at least one of them was going to regret.

She turned toward Lance, her hand on his chest as if to keep him in place. "She's really getting thirsty for that cider—" Melanie shot a quick look toward the stranger "—and I had the distinct impression when I just spoke to her that she was waiting for someone." It was a lie, but the only thing she could come up with at a moment's notice. It was either that or run for cover. She offered the stranger a smile. "Why don't you come in out of the dark?"

The man walked away from his car and into the garage. "I've been trying to do that for a while now."

"Maybe you should have thought of that before you left," Lance bit off.

With that he shrugged Melanie's hand away and walked back into the house, leaving her stunned in his wake.

The older man joined her. "You'll have to excuse him," he said quietly. "I'm not exactly his favorite person right now. I haven't been for quite some time, not that I can really blame him." He lifted his shoulders in a half shrug. "I guess Bess didn't tell him that she was inviting me."

"It's her party. I don't think she has to clear the guest list with him."

Melanie turned around to look at the man. In the light, the resemblance was even more pronounced, more uncanny. The man wore a dark, well-trimmed mustache, but the cheekbones, the shape of the nose, the strong jaw, they were all Lance.

She realized that she was staring and flashed him an apologetic look. "I didn't know Lance had an older brother. I thought he was an only child."

He laughed softly, but there was a sadness to the sound.

"He is, and I think I'm really going to like you." He put his hand out. "I'm Lance's father, Bruce. Bess's baby brother." There was a time when that description had annoyed him, but now it merely tickled him to say it. There was twenty years between them, and he'd always thought of Bess more as his mother than his sister.

"Lance's father?" Melanie echoed. The man looked much too young to have a son as old as Lance. "He never mentioned a father."

"I'm not surprised. Things have been strained between us for a very long time. My fault." Bruce looked toward the doorway with deep regret. All his attempts at a reconciliation in the past few years had failed. "But he won't let me make amends. Stubborn."

The smile returned again. It was, Melanie thought, a very nice smile. The same smile that she'd glimpsed occasionally on Lance's lips. She had to find a way to coax it out again.

"Like me," Bruce added. He tucked the gift he'd brought for Bess under his arm and opened the door for Melanie. "But we shouldn't be standing here, talking in the garage. Lance might get the wrong idea."

She sincerely doubted that Lance would care one way of the other. "Lance doesn't have any ideas when it comes to me," she said with regret.

Bruce raised a brow just the way she'd seen Lance do.

"Bess never raised any idiots," he told her. And then he thought better of his testimony. He'd lost his wife, decades too early, through no fault of his own. And in the bargain he'd managed to lose his son, too. But that had been his fault, and he meant to change that any way he could. "Except, maybe one."

He meant himself. Something else she wanted to find out about, Melanie thought as she crossed the threshold into the house once again.

The warmth within the house was in direct contrast to the frost she saw in Lance's eyes when she entered.

"If you'll excuse me?" she murmured to Bruce, already beginning to make her way to Lance.

"Your father seems very nice," she told Lance. Out of the corner of her eye, she saw Bruce greet Bess with a quick hug.

Lance shrugged, feigning disinterest. Why hadn't he just stayed away? It was what his father was good at, Lance thought. "Some people think so."

She studied his profile. It was so unyieldingly rigid, she could have ironed on it. "But you don't."

He was in no mood to discuss it. It was only because he knew it would upset Bess that he didn't just walk out. But that didn't mean he had to put up with an amateur psychologist.

"Don't try to analyze me, McCloud." Wanting to get away from her, from the crowded house, he went out on the patio.

Melanie followed him. She stood her ground, even though he sounded ready to bite her head off. "I'm not analyzing, I'm asking questions and trying to understand what's going on."

Lance shoved his hands into his pockets, staring up at the sky, trying to get in control of his anger. Why did he still let it get to him like this?

"Why?" he demanded. "Why does it matter to you?"

"Because it just does, that's all." She swung him around until he had to look at her. "*You* matter to me, okay?"

No, it wasn't okay. It wasn't okay at all. Hearing her say it just messed with his head. He was trying his damnedest not to let her get to him. But his damnedest wasn't good enough.

He sighed. "What's going on is that my father thinks he can just come back into my life, say he made a mistake and expect everything to be the way it was fifteen years ago. Well, it can't."

She nodded her head solemnly. "You've gotten taller for one thing."

"Don't make a joke out of this," he warned.

"I'm only trying to lighten your mood," she told him gently. "It's your aunt's birthday, and you look as if thunderbolts could come shooting out of your brows at any minute." She laid her hand on his arm in a silent entreaty. He was letting this eat him up. "Whatever he did, it's in the past. There's your whole future to think of. Do you want it to be just like this moment, full of anger and hurt?"

He didn't want to be lectured to, even for the best of reasons. She didn't understand what he'd been through, not any of it. "You think you know everything? How would you feel if your father walked out on you and never looked back?"

She didn't miss a beat. "He did," she told him quietly. "And I forgave him for it a long time ago. There was no point in hating him. It was only hurting me, not to mention my mother."

Lance looked at her, stunned. He could've kicked himself, if it was anatomically possible.

Blowing out a long breath, he dragged his hand through his hair. "Hey, I didn't mean—" He wasn't any good at apologies, never had been. "Look, I'm a jerk." The laugh was harsh and self-deprecating. "But you should already know that."

She touched his face, making him look at her. Making

him look into her eyes. What he saw scared him. Because he wanted it so much.

"No, I don't," Melanie told him. "Because you're not. You're a little hotheaded and you're probably vying for the honor of being selected as the poster boy for the word *brooding*, but you're definitely not a jerk, Lance."

She was unbelievable. He began feeling the anger, the tension, draining from him. "Why do you always try to put the best spin on things?"

"Because the alternative is very depressing, and I don't like being depressed for more than two hours." She saw he didn't understand. "That's about the time it takes to watch the uncut version of *Stella Dallas*." She grinned. "Ten hankies, no waiting."

He threw back his head and looked up at the sky. It was completely dark. A new moon and no stars. Just like his soul had felt a few minutes ago.

But not now, he realized. Lance looked at her, awed by the change she could make without even trying. "I'm not like you, Melanie."

He'd called her by her first name. She liked the sound of it on his tongue. She refrained from commenting, knowing that would sound the death knell. "I'm beginning to realize that. Doesn't mean you have to live in a black hole for the rest of your life."

He shook his head, the slightest hint of a smile playing on his lips. "Nothing lives in a black hole."

"My point exactly." She tucked her arm through his and began to lead him back inside. "Why don't you return to that armed truce you had with your father for the time being and let Bess blow out her candles in peace?"

How was it that she managed to keep guessing ac-

curately about him, as if she could somehow look into
his soul? "What makes you think there was a truce?"

"Because—" she stepped into the living room, moving the sliding glass door back into place "—Bess
wouldn't have invited all these people to watch the two
of you fight it out." Melanie guessed that in some ways
Bess was as private as her nephew was. "And besides,
I heard the two of you 'talking' before I opened the
garage door." She turned to look at him. "There was
enough frost coming from you to decorate the set of the
winter carnival scene in *Shine On, Harvest Moon.*"

He could only shake his head. "Does everything re-
mind you of a movie?"

"Pretty much." She decided to play it up for his benefit. "So, are you willing to forgo reenacting the cli-
mactic gunfight scene from *Gunfight at OK Corral* for
the time being?"

He considered the comparison. "More like the last
gunfight in *High Noon* since there's just two of us and
not a crowd.

She looked at him in surprise, a wide smile he wanted
to kiss away forming. "Why, Lance, I'm very im-
pressed. You did watch movies."

"Some," he conceded. "With Bess." It was for her
sake that he decided to rein in his feelings. Hers and
Melanie's. Somehow—though he wasn't exactly certain
just how—Melanie had defused the hostility he felt.

"I've got a huge collection of videos," she told him
as they watched one of Bess's friends come out with the
cake.

"Why doesn't that surprise me?"

She'd meant it as an opening line. If he'd watched old
movies as a boy, maybe he'd want to see some of them

again. "Maybe you'd like to come over and watch something with me sometime."

"Maybe," he said.

The conversation was curtailed as everyone began to sing "Happy Birthday." But there was no curtailing the smile that was blooming on Melanie's face.

Chapter Ten

Okay, maybe he was asking for trouble.

Lance frowned as he stood before the narrow door that was just to the left of the entrance to Melanie's shop.

The lights in the shop itself were out. Dreams of Yesterday was closed. It had been for the past hour and a half. Twilight tiptoed around the street behind him, careful not to disturb anything as the city settled down for the night.

He wasn't settling down. He felt as restless as a cat standing in front of a pet shop filled with dogs. Lance shook his head. Even the simplest fool knew enough to get out of the way of an oncoming truck before getting flattened. And he was no fool.

Yeah, he was.

Otherwise he wouldn't be standing there, in front of her private entrance, with some lame excuse bouncing around in his brain. It went further than that. If he wasn't a fool, he wouldn't have sent her those flowers, either.

He would have just seen the threat she posed to him and kept on going.

And she did pose a threat. A very real threat to the life he'd painstakingly reconstructed for himself. Why the hell was he jeopardizing that by seeking her out this way?

He was functioning now, wasn't he? Something he had doubted he could do two years ago when he had lain there in his hospital bed, staring at the ceiling.

Not just because of the injuries to his body. Those he'd always known would heal, even though the doctors initially had their doubts. Scarred flesh would heal, his legs would move. But the other, that was much harder to overcome.

It was the other injury that had stood in his way. The injury to his soul. There was a helplessness that pervaded it. The helplessness that he'd felt when he couldn't save that old woman from the fire.

The helplessness he'd felt watching Lauren walk away, and with her, his last hopes for something better than what he had. An emptiness that invaded every part of his being.

It was the same emptiness that had been there when his father had left him. But then there had been Bess to pull and tug at him until he finally made it back to the surface again. Like a continuing flow of water wearing away the surface of a rock, she'd kept after him until he became a functioning, contributing human being.

The emptiness had been waiting for him after he regained consciousness in the hospital. Waiting like an old dreaded adversary biding its time until it could vanquish him. But somehow, maybe it was strength of character, maybe it was stubbornness, he'd pulled through again. Not as well as the first time, but he'd risen above the emptiness enough to get back to work, to find something he was still good at and then do it.

But if there was a third battle, Lance wasn't sure he could survive it. He wasn't sure he wanted to. Because if he gambled, if he let this woman into his life, let her affect him so that there was a glimmer of hope again, and then she walked out on him, what would there be left of him to continue?

If he let her into his life...

If?

What *if*? he mocked silently. She was already there. If she wasn't, he wouldn't be standing here, staring at her doorbell, calling himself seven kinds of a fool for wanting to ring it.

"I haven't got it fine-tuned for mind control yet. You still have to ring it yourself."

The sound of her voice made him jump. Lance looked around, wondering if he'd imagining it, the way he'd been imagining her this past week.

"Up here." Stepping back on the sidewalk, Lance saw her. She was leaning out of the second-floor window. Even in the dim illumination from the street lamp, he could see the amusement on her face. "I saw your car in the street."

Mechanically he looked behind him. As if he didn't know where his car was, he thought, annoyed with his lack of aplomb.

"I, um..."

Now what did he say? That he'd been thinking of her ever since Bess's party last week? That he'd tried not to, but couldn't seem to be able to weed her out of his thoughts?

He thought of his excuse. It was still lame, but it was all he had. "I came by to pay you."

"Wait right there," she told him.

Fairly flying down the stairs in her bare feet, Melanie made it to the ground floor in record time. She knew if she didn't hurry, Lance might just leave as mysteriously as he had come. When she'd gone to the window to shut it and spotted him, he looked like a deer trapped in the headlights of an oncoming car. A deer that was going to bolt at any minute. It wasn't a stretch for her to guess that he didn't like being caught like this. Vulnerable.

She had no idea what payment he was referring to, but she didn't care. Lance was here. After five days, she'd almost given up hope that he'd turn up. Almost.

Yanking open the door, she let go of the breath she was holding. He was still there, thank God, looking very much as if he doubted his own sanity. "Pay me for what?"

He dug his hands deep into his pockets. "For the photograph." He headed off her protest before she had a chance to utter it. "I know you said you didn't want to take any money, but I don't feel as if I gave Bess the gift if I don't pay you for it."

It made perfectly logical sense. So why did he feel as if she could see right through it? As if she knew it was just an excuse to her as well as himself so he could see her again.

Melanie didn't want his money. She'd given the photograph to him as a gift, which he'd been free to pass on to his aunt. It didn't feel right, going back on the bargain.

"I told you, it's priceless."

Now that he'd given her the excuse, he wasn't about to just shrug and walk away. She'd think him an idiot. Odds were she did, anyway, he thought, and she was probably right.

Lance remained impassive. "Come up with something."

It'd be a lot easier if he just learned to graciously accept things. Melanie pressed her lips together, thinking. And then she smiled.

"All right. I said that you couldn't put a price on it, but before people used money, they bartered for things."

Lance didn't like the light that had come into her eyes. He had a bad feeling about this. "You want me to barter?"

She rocked forward on her bare toes. "No, but I do have an offer to make you."

He glanced down and saw that she wasn't wearing any shoes. That would explain why she looked even smaller and more delicate. Exactly like one of those china dolls Bess used to collect, he thought.

A doll with a will of iron. "I'm listening," he said slowly.

She opened the door wider, inviting him in. "If you really want to pay for the photograph, come upstairs with me now."

He tried to second-guess her and failed. Just what was she asking for? "Why?"

Was he always so suspicious about everything? she wondered. Or was it just her he held suspect?

"I was just about to put *Rebecca* into my VCR. I'd rather watch movies with someone than by myself. You can keep me company."

He'd come here wanting to be with her. But now that she was inviting him in, he hesitated, knowing what could happen if he crossed the threshold. He felt as if his self-control was just hanging by the barest of threads as it was.

"Well, I..."

"Got a hot date waiting?"

"No."

He said it with such feeling, she almost laughed. Was a date really such an awful thing for him to contemplate? "Then you're free." She cocked her head, waiting. "That's my price, take it or leave it."

He stood there, debating, knowing he should be turning on his heel and walking toward his car if he had even the slightest use of his brain still available to him.

"I'll take it," he finally said.

She'd known he would. Well, at least ninety-three percent of her had known. But it was pretty much a sure thing. If it hadn't been, he wouldn't have shown up here to begin with. What Lance wanted was to be pushed in the right direction. Lucky for him, being covertly pushy was her specialty.

"Great." Melanie linked her fingers with his and drew him inside. His expression was no longer dark, just wary. "Smile, Lance. It's a movie, not an execution."

He wasn't so sure about that.

The apartment above her shop was warm and cozy. It suited her, he thought looking around. What surprised him was that it wasn't an extension of the shop downstairs. There was no preponderance of autographed, framed photos on the walls, no clutter of movie memorabilia lying around on every flat surface in the room. It was all neat and tidy and pleasingly spacious.

"What happened?" He made himself comfortable on the gray-blue leather sofa. It went beyond comfort. He felt as if he was being embraced by an old friend. "This looks like a normal living room. Did you run out of movie material?"

"Not quite." A grin played on her lips. "You're sitting in the middle of the living room set from 'Dad's Home.'" It was obvious from his expression that he didn't know what she was talking about. "It was a popular sitcom that ran for seven seasons in the eighties." She bent down in front of the VCR beneath the TV and inserted the tape. "This was their living room."

He might have known. "How did it get to be your living room?"

"Not mine, Aunt Elaine's." She'd just inherited it. Setting the video cover aside on the table, she moved the remote closer to his side and rose. "It was the last show she worked on." Melanie walked out to the kitchen. "The executive producer, who was also the star, had a soft spot in his heart for Aunt Elaine." Her voice floated back to him. He heard the refrigerator door being opened, then closed. Juggling two cans of soda, napkins and a bowl of popcorn, Melanie reentered the room. "She'd kind of taken him under her wing when he was starting out—"

She was going to drop something. Why didn't she just make two trips? That would be the logical thing to do. But he was beginning to learn that Melanie and logic did not belong in the same sentence. Getting up, Lance met her halfway and took the cans from her, setting them on the coffee table.

"What, did she show him how to dress?" It was a flippant remark, and he was surprised when Melanie actually validated it. But he shouldn't have been. It was becoming apparent to him that the whole family was offbeat.

"Pretty much. David Matthews had no eye for style at all. She dressed him, advanced him a little money when he needed it and introduced him to a few people she knew, who in turn introduced him to a few others and so on." Melanie placed the pile of napkins between them, setting the bowl down. "He never forgot what she did for him and, since she admired the set, when the show went off the air, he gave it to her as a gift."

She said it as if it was the most natural thing in the world. As if everyone's living room furniture came fresh off a movie lot. "Did your kitchen come courtesy of 'Cooking with Julia Child?'"

She laughed. Well, at least he knew the name of one program. "No, but my bedroom is from *1,001 Arabian Nights.*"

The grin on her face was infectious and tempting. He caught himself wanting to sample it firsthand. For his sake, he hoped the movie was going to be short.

"I had the greatest childhood a girl could possibly imagine." She'd spent hours in her room, fantasizing. Being rescued by a dark, handsome warrior, whose face changed periodically, depending on who she had a crush on that week.

Melanie pushed the popcorn bowl in his direction. A few of the kernels bailed out onto the rug, and she bent over to pick them up. The pink-and-white top she was wearing hadn't looked as if it was cut low until she bent over. The view he was treated to left him just a little weak.

Lance had to force himself to look away, but it wasn't easy.

She dusted off her hands, then reached for the remote. "So, are you ready to pay up?"

Distracted, he blinked, trying to focus on what she was saying and not on how firm and ripe her breasts appeared to be. He felt his palms itch and dug them into the sofa on either side of him. Out of harm's way.

"What?"

Oblivious to what she was doing to him, Melanie wiggled into the sofa to make herself comfortable.

"The movie." Pointing the remote at the screen, she asked, "Are you ready to watch it? *Rebecca* is a real classic."

He groaned as he shifted on the sofa. To her that sounded far from promising. "Does that mean I'm going to fall asleep?" he asked.

He obviously didn't know anything about the movie, or that it was a mystery. Melanie curled up against the cushion, tucking her feet under her. There were few things she loved more than watching a good movie. "I doubt it."

So did he, he decided, slanting a glance at her. People rarely fell asleep when they were as tense as he was.

Beautifully lettered credits inched their way dramatically up the screen as the background faded away. He'd eaten too much popcorn, Lance thought. But it had been a defensive move meant to keep his hands busy. And away from her.

Brushing a kernel casing from his hands, Lance could feel her eyes on him. She was waiting for him to say something.

"That wasn't half-bad," he said. In fact, he added silently, it'd been far more entertaining than he'd thought it would be.

"Not half-bad?" She supposed in his language he was giving it a five-star review, but it did deserve a little more than just a nonnegative comment. "It was wonderful." Melanie aimed the remote in the general direction of the set and pressed Rewind. "Tell me, has anything ever gotten an unqualified, enthusiastic seal of approval from you?"

He couldn't begin to think of the last time he'd been enthusiastic about something. Even his work. He did it to the best of his ability, but enthusiasm? That didn't figure into it.

The only time he'd felt even the most remote stirring of enthusiasm was while he was kissing her.

"No," he snapped.

The denial was almost physical in its force. Her guess was that he had and didn't want to think about it or even admit it.

"How about Bess?" she asked.

"She's a person, not a thing." He shrugged, allowing her to stretch the definition. He would never deny having feelings for Bess. "And if it weren't for her, I wouldn't be sitting here, remember?"

The present, right. "I remember." Looking at the table, she debated cleaning up and decided to leave it. There was time enough for that when he left. "So, only Bess? No one else?"

Was she fishing for a compliment? It didn't seem like her, but then, just how much did he really know about this woman? "Should there be?"

Her answer caught him completely off guard. "Your father."

The mild expression faded. "Don't you start. I get enough of that from Bess." And even she couldn't get him to come around. What made McCloud think that she could persuade him?

Melanie raised her hands in innocent surrender. "I'm not starting."

Yes, she was, but she figured now wasn't the best time to admit that. In her heart she really believed that Lance needed more than just a cease-fire between him and Bruce. He needed his father back.

"All right, what would you call it?"

"Taking an interest in you."

Lance already knew she was good at talking her way out of things, but it wasn't going to work this time. He knew what she was trying to do, and he wanted her to stop.

"Well, don't. Take up a hobby instead." Lance gestured at the TV set just as the VCR stopped rewinding, retiring with a loud click. "Go watch another movie."

It was the perfect out, but she didn't want to back away from the subject. There came a time when you had to face things, when you had to risk a friend's displeasure for their own good. For her, that time came now.

She placed her hand on his arm, silently imploring him to listen to reason. "You're letting this eat at you and that's not healthy. Your father wants to make up, Lance. He wants to get back into your life."

"What, did he tell you that?" Had his father played on her sympathies last week? Had he painted himself as the wronged victim? Lance's mouth hardened. "Did he ask you to act as go-between? I can't believe—"

Her hands on both sides of his face, she made Lance look at her before he could continue with his denouncement.

"No, he didn't," Melanie said forcefully. "He didn't say anything except that he was the one to blame for all this."

Just the tiniest bit of his anger abated with the admission. "Well, he was right there."

This wasn't about right and wrong, she thought. It was about feelings. And until he could let go of the bad ones, he wouldn't be free to allow the good ones to come. He wouldn't be free to love anyone.

"All right, so if he admits that, why go on punishing him?" Her eyes searched his. "And yourself?"

How could she ask him just to forget everything? Forget that his father walked out on him when he needed him most?

Annoyed, he rose. He was halfway to the door before he swung around again, an accusing look in his eyes. "You above all people should understand. You can't tell me that you didn't wonder why your father walked out on you, that you didn't spend sleepless nights thinking that maybe it was something you did or said that made him leave." He drew a breath, letting it out slowly. The tension, the anger didn't abate. "That there was something so damn bad about you that no one wanted to stick around, not even your own father."

Oh, God, was that what he'd thought? Her heart ached for the pain he'd lived with as a child.

"Sometimes people do things that have nothing to do with anyone else. They don't even realize that their action is hurting someone. They just know how much they're hurting themselves." She looked at him, hoping she was getting through on some level. "I think you have more in common with your father than you think."

Because she'd come closer to the truth than he was willing to admit, Lance turned away and walked toward the door without saying anything. He didn't trust himself to be rational, and once said, things couldn't be taken back.

Melanie was in front of him in a heartbeat. She didn't want him leaving this way. "You asked how I felt about my father not being there. All right, I'll tell you." Her eyes held his. "I knew it wasn't anything I said or did, because he left before I was born. He left because of my very existence." And it had hurt something awful, but she'd dealt with it and put it all behind her, neatly wrapped, so to speak. For his sake, she undid the carefully wrapped package. "My father didn't even stay around to find out if I was a boy or girl, if I was healthy or not. If I needed anything. If my mother needed anything."

That had hurt her the most, that this wonderful woman who was her mother had had her heart broken by someone she'd loved. Melanie took a breath, as if that helped hold the pain of the memory back somehow.

"Over the years he never even tried to get in contact with me or my mother. He didn't want to have any part of us." She saw what she took to be pity in his eyes and accepted it the way it was meant. It heartened her that he could feel for her, or at least relate.

"I guess that's why I loved Aunt Elaine's world so much. One week I could pretend that Danny Thomas was my father, the next it was Brian Keith. It was always some warm, wonderful, father figure who was guaranteed to love me no matter what my faults were." She shrugged. "Pretending helped."

Maybe it'd helped her, but he saw it as just a crutch. "I don't live in a world of make-believe, McCloud. I never did."

All right, she would meet him on his level.

"Well, the reality is that if I could somehow find my father, I would. Not to ask him how he could have left me, but to ask him if he wanted to stay now. If he wanted to make the most of the time we have left." She looked at him pointedly, wishing she knew how to get through to him. "You're the lucky one. You don't have to search for your father. He's right there. And he wants to be your father again. I'd give anything to be in your shoes." She caught his arm as he turned from her. "Yesterday's gone, Lance. It's a dream. All we have is today. Do something with it that you won't regret down the road. There've been enough regrets, don't you think?''

"I think you talk too much." But the edge was gone from his voice.

"Maybe at times," she admitted, her eyes on his. "Because I care."

He still didn't understand. After all, it wasn't as if he'd made any effort to start something between them. Just the opposite was true.

"Why?"

She shook her head. She had no substantial answer to his question. It wasn't a matter of solving an equation. It was just something that was.

"We don't pick the people we care about, Lance. We just do." She nodded toward the television set. There was news playing in the background now. "Are you up for another movie?"

"I've got an early day tomorrow."

It was an excuse. He knew if he stayed any longer he wouldn't be leaving at all tonight. And he wasn't ready to take that step, no matter how much he wanted to. Not yet. Because with her, it wouldn't be casual. Not for either of them. And he didn't want her getting hurt.

She accompanied him to the door. Feeling awkward, he kissed her lightly on the cheek. "Thanks for the movie education."

A sweetness filtered through her as she brushed her fingers along her cheek. "Anytime. No charge."

Unable to help himself, he watched her mouth as she spoke. Temptation tugged at him, and he struggled to resist.

She was wrong, he thought. There was a charge. And the price was his soul.

"See you," he murmured. Leaving before he changed his mind and couldn't.

Chapter Eleven

A small woman with what Lance figured had to be the world's pointiest elbows drove one into his side as she tried to get him to move. She was angling for a better view of one of the displays Melanie had laid out in her shop.

The shop was full of people, mostly women, all of whom had been invited to a tea to celebrate the fiftieth anniversary of *The Thief of Hearts,* a movie he'd never even heard of. But Bess had.

It was because of Bess he was here. He'd been roped into coming. But, he supposed, he really had no one to blame but himself. If he hadn't mentioned the tea to Bess, when he'd been trying to keep Melanie from attending her party, Bess wouldn't have known about it. Bess never forgot anything. So when the date rolled around, she'd called him up and asked if he wanted to accompany her to the shop, seeing as she didn't know where it was and he did.

If Bess thought she was fooling him, he had news for

her. He knew of few women who were as independent as she was. She didn't need him to show her where the shop was. Bess just wanted him to come along so that she could throw him together with McCloud again.

No matter how he tried, Lance thought as he moved out of the forceful customer's elbow range, his path kept crossing McCloud's, willingly or otherwise.

Out of boredom he glanced at a tag to see how much she was asking for the dress he found himself pushed up against. He blinked twice to make sure he wasn't seeing things. Was she serious?

"Found something you like?"

He looked up into Melanie's amused expression. "Do people really *pay* prices like this?" Lance held up the small tag that Joy had written out and attached to the sleeve of a deep green velvet gown. The gown looked too damn heavy to maneuver around in. Who in their right mind would even *want* it? "I mean, this is four figures."

"You'd be surprised." Melanie smoothed out a wrinkle in the skirt. "People pay a lot for nostalgia."

There was nostalgia and then there was insanity, he thought. "Apparently." He let go of the tag, still shaking his head. "You'd really be doing well for yourself if you weren't always giving the merchandise away."

She couldn't quite read his expression. Was he mocking her or only making a casual observation? No, she amended, it might have been an observation, but there was nothing casual about Lance. There was an intensity just beneath the surface no matter what he did or said. It was part of his sensual appeal.

"I don't always give it away," she told him. "Just at my discretion."

Lance hadn't a clue as to how McCloud's mind

worked, only that it was so totally unconventional that any guess he made would turn out to be wrong. "And that would be…?"

She looked at him, for a moment forgetting everyone else in the crowded store. The turnout was even larger than she'd hoped for. It looked as if every single customer she'd ever sold anything to had shown up. Luckily in shifts, but the store was still jammed. Thank God she'd thought to take on extra people to help with the sales.

"When my heart tells me to." A playful smile alleviated the serious moment. "But my body likes to eat, so it doesn't let my heart do too much talking."

He laughed shortly. "I wouldn't have thought you had a logical bone in you." Just a soft, sweet body he was acutely aware of being far too close for him to ignore indefinitely.

"Personally I find logic to be very overrated." She cocked her head, studying him. His features had softened a little. She wondered if that was because he was here with Bess, or if, just maybe, she was getting to him a little. "Do you ever listen to your heart, Lance?"

Now *that* was an overrated entity. All it did was lead you into trouble. "Only to see if it's beating or not."

Because he wanted something to do with his hands before he gave in to the very strong impulse that was drumming through him, he picked up a white satin mask that was lying on the counter. There was no tag on it.

He held the mask up to her. "How much is this?"

She lowered her eyes to the item, then raised them again. He could almost feel her look feathering along his face. His gut tightened like a fist.

"For you?"

If he were asking for favors from her, they wouldn't

involve something so inconsequential as a white mask. "For anyone."

Melanie looked at it again, trying to remember what she and Joy had agreed on. "Two hundred and fifty dollars."

He let out a low whistle. "Seems kind of steep don't you think?" There was only a little bit of material involved. It was the kind of mask worn over a person's eyes. Like Zorro, he thought, if Zorro had favored white. "Ski masks are going for fifteen dollars, and they cover a lot more. Halloween masks for less."

She laughed, taking it from him and carefully arranging it again on the counter. "It's not the mask, it's what it represents. This was the mask Juliet wore when she first saw Romeo in the Julian Rogers movie version of the play. Did you see it?" He gave her a look that said she had to be kidding. She laughed in response. "You're right, what was I thinking?"

Her laugh went right through him, burrowing deep into his belly. Conspiring with her scent, it was undoing him at a rapid rate. He looked around for a means of escape. Maybe he'd just find Bess and tell her he'd wait for her in the car until she had her fill of this place.

He'd probably be sitting there until Christmas if he worded it that way, he thought darkly.

He didn't have to find Bess. She found him, although it was clear that the object of her search was Melanie. Her round face was flushed, not just from the close quarters, but with pleasure. She took Melanie's arm for extra support.

"Melanie, this place is absolutely fabulous. It's like being in wonderland." Her eyes shifted momentarily to her nephew. "Lance, why didn't you tell me about Melanie's shop?"

Thinking quickly, Melanie spared Lance the effort of coming up with an excuse. "Wonderful is in the eyes of the beholder." Even as she worked the floor, she'd watched Bess's progress and her reaction to various items. She never tired of the thrill of seeing the shop for the first time through someone else's eyes. "See anything you like?"

"Everything," Bess breathed. "I feel like I've died and gone to heaven."

Lance shuddered, his eyes shutting out the sight. "Heaven a movie theater. Now there's a frightening thought."

"Only if the popcorn is stale," Melanie quipped. There was a woman impatiently circling the register, looking for a clerk. Melanie squeezed Bess's arm. "If there's something special that catches your eye, let me know. I have to see about a customer, but I'll be right back."

Bess waited long enough for Melanie to be relatively out of earshot. "The special thing that's caught my eye is her."

Lance watched Melanie ring up the sale. She was telling the woman something that made the latter look with awed pleasure at the item she'd just purchased. From where he stood, it looked like a common letter opener. Probably used by some "dashing" leading man to pick his teeth, he thought drily, shaking his head. Melanie was just chock-full of stories.

"Yeah," he agreed, distracted, "she's something, all right."

If he'd have let her, Bess would have hugged him. But Lance hated displays of affection in public. Still, it didn't diminish the relief she felt. He was finally coming around. "Well, at least you noticed. It's a start."

Her words penetrated after a beat. Lance looked at her sharply. "Just as long as *you* don't start, Bess." He didn't have to guess was going on in her head. He knew Bess too well. "Things are fine just the way they are."

"No," Bess disagreed firmly, "they're not. And the sooner you admit that, the sooner you can go on with your life. I didn't raise you to become a bitter old man years before your time."

The affection he bore for Bess made him smile at her declaration. "When *can* I become a bitter old man?" he teased.

She sniffed. "When you hit a hundred." With a heavy gait, she moved away from him and toward the armoire that had caught her eye when she had first walked into the shop. She'd returned to it three times now in the past half hour. Each time she did, it looked even better to her than it had the last.

Melanie finished ringing up the sale in time to see the expression on Bess's face. She knew unabashed love when she saw it.

Another customer tried to get her attention, but she tactfully turned her over to Joy and made her way back to Bess. Lance's aunt was running her hand lovingly over the highly polished finish.

They were made for each other, Melanie thought. "So, this catch your fancy?"

Bess nodded, hardly able to tear her eyes away. The hand carved piece was decorated with the likeness of a man and a woman looking longingly at each other. When the doors were opened, they parted. It was deliciously romantic.

"It's from *Robin's Woman*, isn't it?" Bess sighed. "I must have seen that movie a dozen times. Robin hides in here until Maid Marian comes into the room and goes to bed.''

The romance of that eluded Lance, who had just walked over. ''Sounds like someone they'd arrest for being a Peeping Tom these days,'' he pointed out.

The bald statement left Bess stymied. ''Where did I go wrong with you?''

Taking her arm, Melanie subtly turned her back to the armoire. ''Men don't like admitting that they're romantic,'' she told the older woman. ''Doesn't seem quite masculine to them to feel like that. But they do, deep down.''

She said it with way too much conviction to suit him, Lance thought. As if she thought she could read him as easily as a want ad. Well, she couldn't.

Could she?

Ignoring her, he ran his hand along the curved piece. ''At least it's sturdy.'' The fact surprised him.

Melanie heartily agreed. ''It had to be. Jean-Luc Delon spent the better part of a whole day crouching in it. I think they reshot that one scene thirty-seven times. He threatened to burn the armoire when the movie was over.'' Melanie unlocked the doors for Bess and showed her the armoire's interior. ''Fortunately he got sidetracked.''

Bess nodded, getting into the spirit of the story. ''Allison Evans.''

''His third wife.'' Melanie smiled, remembering. ''Broke a lot of hearts that summer when he got married.''

He had no idea who the hell John Luke was. But he picked up on her tone and he didn't like it. And he liked even less that it bothered him. ''Yours?''

Melanie nodded. She made no effort to deny it.

"Mine." And then, because she saw the expression on his face, an expression she knew he would have been horrified to discover he was wearing, she added, "I was eight."

"Oh." He shrugged as if it didn't matter to him one way or the other. It annoyed him that it did, but McCloud didn't have to know that.

Throughout the exchange, Bess had been debating with herself and arrived at a decision. "I'll take it," she announced.

She reached for the price tag. Melanie was faster and ripped it off before Bess had a chance to see it.

"All right," Melanie said cheerfully. "I'll just ring it up for you."

Now that she had made her decision, Bess braced herself for the blow. "How much shall I write the check for?"

Melanie never missed a beat as she glanced at the tag and answered, "Five hundred dollars."

Lance's brow rose in mute surprise. He'd taken a look at the tag when he had examined the piece. It was priced at six times that.

Even Bess seemed highly skeptical. "Melanie, dear," she began tactfully, "I'll admit I'm not rolling in money, but I do like to acquire what I get honestly."

Melanie looked at her as if she didn't know what she was talking about. "No, really. It's five hundred. Here, look." Opening her palm, Melanie displayed the tag for Bess's perusal.

Lance looked at it over his aunt's shoulder. The price tag in Melanie's hand was written out for five hundred dollars even. That was cheaper than a department store price. Just what was she up to?

"It's been here ever since I opened the shop. I've

reduced the price a couple of times already, but no one's been interested in it enough to give it a home.'' Melanie frowned at the piece as if it were an annoying relative who was more trouble than he was worth. ''You'd be doing me a favor if you bought it.''

Bess was still doubtful, but she knew when it was futile to argue. Melanie had that in common with Lance, she mused. God help their children.

''Can't resist doing a favor, now, can I?'' Bess looked around the shop for somewhere to sit so she could write the check. ''Now, shall I make the check out to the shop or to you?''

Melanie indicated the chair to her left. John Wayne had sat in it during the filming of *McClintock,* but that was a story for another time.

''The shop.'' She looked at Lance significantly. ''I can deliver it to your place tonight after I close, if I have help.''

If she could practically give the piece away, he could certainly come and help her load it up so she could deliver it.

''You'll have help,'' he assured her grudgingly.

Her eyes sparkled in that annoying, enticing way of hers. ''Lucky for me you're around.''

Luck, he thought, had very little to do with it.

She was a hell of a lot stronger than she looked, Lance thought, slamming the back of the van shut. He tested the doors to make sure they were locked. He'd returned at six-thirty as promised, fully prepared to wrestle with the heavy piece of furniture himself. Melanie had insisted on helping, even when he'd growled at her to stand back.

Ignoring his dismissal, she'd picked up one side, and

between the two of them, they'd gotten it into the van, if not with ease, at least without the maximum effort he'd expected. Hopping up inside, she quickly tied the armoire down so that it wouldn't move around within the van when they drove.

The woman was just one surprise after another.

"I might have known," Lance muttered, climbing into the passenger side of her van.

She waited until he'd slid the seat belt into place before turning on the ignition. "Known what?" She backed up slowly until she was out of the space and easing onto the street.

"That that slightly blue haze I noticed coming from under your blouse was your superheroine costume." He rolled down the window, unwilling to sit in a sealed compartment with her perfume seducing him. "Can you fly, too, along with having super strength?"

Melanie just barely squeaked through the light. She glanced in her rearview mirror to make sure there were no police cars in the vicinity—just in case. "You're exaggerating."

He drummed his fingers along the rim of the open window. "I wasn't aware that you could tell the difference."

Melanie pushed her hair away from her face. The breeze challenged her for control, whipping it back into her eyes. She moved it aside again.

"It's all in the leverage," she explained. "The gaffers who set up the scenes on the set taught me that." She spared him a glance. He wasn't really talking about getting the armoire into the van. "What's this about?"

Because Bess had been around earlier, he hadn't gotten the chance to ask her. He asked now. "I want to know how you managed to turn a three-thousand-dollar price tag into one that said five hundred.''

''Oh, that.'' She'd almost forgotten about that. ''Would you believe magic?'

A few weeks ago he would have told her what she could do with that explanation. Now, however, he was having doubts about the way he perceived things.

''I'm beginning to.''

He looked at her for a moment, then looked away. This was getting bad. He found himself wanting her all the time. Maybe it was just a matter of wanting something that he couldn't have. Maybe if he did have her, the mystery, the urge would go away and leave him in peace. It was worth thinking about.

No, thinking about making love with her was only going to make it worse.

He was making himself crazy.

''And that's what worries me,'' he added.

She gave him a break and explained. ''Actually, it comes back to leverage, just a different kind. Sleight of hand, Lance.'' The reference meant nothing to him. ''I had another price tag in my hand. I wrote it out when I saw the way she was looking at the armoire. I knew she couldn't afford it.'' She glanced at him. ''Remember the dalmatian I gave you?''

The light dawned. ''The one that wound up in my pocket even when I said I didn't want it.''

His bravado had less conviction to it than before. He didn't believe the denial himself anymore, either, Melanie thought. ''You wanted it. You just didn't want anything from me. At the time.''

It irked him that she thought she had his number. Never mind that there was a chance she might be right. ''What I want from you, McCloud, is to be left alone.''

Melanie didn't even blink an eye. "You don't mean that."

He sighed, temporarily surrendering. She was being nice to Bess, and he didn't feel like arguing with her. "No, I don't, but it was worth a shot saying it." He studied her profile. It was a soft, delicate face that begged for a man's hand. His hand.

Lance curled his fingers in his lap. "Is that how you operate? You keep after people until you wear them down?"

"Usually I just have to smile at them." Turning a corner, she spared him a look. And a smile to illustrate her point. "You're a tougher case. But you know what they say."

He didn't bother suppressing the groan. "No, but I have a feeling I'm going to find out whether I want to or not."

He was learning. "The more effort you put into getting something, the more you treasure it when you finally get it." And she wanted to get to be part of his life, even if it meant just being on the perimeter. "You're not fooling me, you know, Lance Reed."

He couldn't decide if he thought she was adorable or just a pain in the butt. Probably a little of both. "I wasn't aware that I was trying to."

"Then maybe it's yourself you're trying to fool, but it's not working. Inside that hard, blustery exterior is a soft center." And she was going to go on mining until she reached it.

The description had him scowling. Did she think she could sum him up that easily? "I'm not a Tootsie Roll Pop, McCloud."

Melanie just gave him a knowing smile. "Have it your way."

Sometimes retreat was called for before complete annihilation struck. Lance sank down in his seat. "Not so's you'd notice," he murmured. He had a strong hunch that very few people had their way around McCloud unless she wanted them to.

Laughing, Melanie turned down one of Bedford's two main thoroughfares, taking the tree-lined, four-lane road that led to Bess's house.

A dark formation on the horizon caught her attention. It was too small to be a cloud. She glanced toward Lance, but he was looking out the window on his side.

"Lance?"

He heard the uncertain note in her voice. Now what? "Yeah?"

"That dark cloud hanging in the sky over there." She squinted, trying to get a better view herself. It was dreary out, and darkness was drawing in, making it difficult to see. "Is that smoke?"

Every fiber of his being came instantly alive. He looked out the windshield. "Where?"

She pointed. "There."

It was a small, darkening plume just above the cluster of trees. The trees obstructed his view. At this distance, it hardly seemed bigger than the fluffed-up tail of a Persian cat. He craned his neck out the window just as they came to a break in the trees.

"Damn." It was smoke all right. Coming from the residential area.

The plume was gaining in size as she drove toward it. An uneasy premonition wafted through her.

"Do you think that's anywhere near Bess's house?"

"Drive faster," was his only response. A sick feeling was curling through his belly, growing in direct relationship to the widening gray cloud.

Her heart hammering in her chest, Melanie pressed down on the accelerator. The speedometer jumped as she flew through a light that was a split second from red. Taking a corner, she guided the van with the ease of someone who was accustomed to defensive driving.

Had he not been so worried about Bess, he would have asked Melanie where she'd learned to drive like that, but all he could think of, all he could do, was pray that Bess wasn't in danger and that it wasn't her house that was on fire.

But it was.

Lance saw the smoke hovering greedily around the structure as Melanie turned the van onto Bess's block. Located at the end, with no neighbors on three sides of it, the house normally attracted little to no attention. There was no one now to notice the fire that was swiftly marshaling control over the two-story building.

It wasn't a fiery inferno yet, but Lance knew how quickly the situation could change. Perspiration broke out over his brow. Bess loved having a good, roaring fire in the fireplace.

"Damn it, I told her to have that chimney cleaned." He cursed roundly. "Pound on one of the neighbor's doors and call this in," he ordered, leaping out of the van before Melanie had brought it to a full stop.

Running, he left the passenger door hanging open. It almost snapped off as Melanie brought the van to a screeching halt. The vehicle fishtailed before finally stopping.

Melanie yanked on the emergency brake. "Where are you going?" she shouted after him.

"To get Bess. Call!" he ordered.

The doorknob was too hot for him to turn. Heat was radiating through the spaces, daring him to enter. Lance stripped off his windbreaker, wrapping it quickly around his hand and arm. Swinging hard, he drove his arm through the glass in the living room window.

Melanie turned to rush to a neighbor's house when she saw the silver car parked across the street. She recognized it immediately.

Oh, my God.

Out of the corner of her eye, Melanie saw someone running out of the house next to Bess's.

"Call the fire department," she shouted to them as she ran to the burning house.

Hesitating only long enough to mumble a prayer, Melanie climbed in after Lance.

Chapter Twelve

Lance had always had a healthy respect for fire.

Fire was something that couldn't be tamed, only temporarily held in check. Two years ago that respect had turned to fear. He thought he was trapped then, as trapped as the old woman he wasn't able to save. Instinct and blind luck had somehow guided him to the only exit left open to him. He'd gotten out, but not whole. He'd been scarred, both in mind and body.

One set of scars healed, the other had only crusted over.

With all his heart Lance wanted to flee from the inferno. Flee and run for cover. But he couldn't allow fear to paralyze him. He had to find Bess. Find her and get her out before the fire wouldn't let either one of them leave.

Flames hissed a ghoulish greeting as he made it over the windowsill. Without his firefighting gear on, he knew he had only minutes, maybe not even that long, to do what had to be done and get the hell out.

He had no idea where to find Bess. She could have been anywhere, in any of the rooms, and the smoke and flames were making it difficult to see. The flames weren't coming in sheets yet, but they would. They would.

Was she upstairs? God, he hoped not. One hand over his nose and mouth, and trying to breathe as little as possible, Lance scanned what he could of the living room as he made his way through it to the staircase.

And then his heart stopped.

Bess was on the floor just beyond the sofa. She was clutching that damned autographed picture he'd given her. Hurrying to her, Lance almost lost his balance as he tripped over something. It took him a moment to realize what it was.

His eyes stinging from the smoke, Lance made out the form of a man.

His father was lying facedown on the floor, only a few feet away from Bess. It wasn't difficult to see he'd been trying to reach her before smoke had overcome him, as well.

The wide ceiling beam above Lance groaned, serving notice. His father was directly under it. Adrenaline pumping in double time, Lance grabbed his father's arm and dragged him away just as the beam came crashing down, cutting the room in half lengthwise. Other beams criss-crossing the vaulted ceiling made similar noises. He had no idea how long before they followed suit.

He had to choose, choose who to save first, who to return for. What if there wasn't enough time to get them both out? What if his choice meant certain death for one of them? The thought tore him apart.

He wasn't filled with anger or with hostile, hurt feelings anymore. He was just a man who didn't want to see his family taken from him.

Most of all, he didn't want to be the one who made the decision of who lived, who died.

But he had to. If he didn't, if he tried to save them both at the same time, then they would all die.

Steeling himself, Lance made his choice.

The fire swirled and swelled surrealistically around Melanie, its flaming red tongues licking close to her body as she fought to keep Lance in sight. Even a few inches could be enough for her to lose him if they were filled with smoke and fire.

"No," she shouted above the groan of the fire. Lance was stooping to pick Bess up. He was going to carry his aunt out first. Melanie jumped over a burning cushion to reach him. Every second counted. "Take your father, I'll take Bess. Your father's too heavy for me."

Stunned at the sound of her voice, Lance whirled around to see Melanie running toward him. "What the—"

"Take him!" she cried, coughing. The smoke was already filling her throat and lungs. They felt as if they were bursting.

Anger flared uncontrollably through him. Had she lost her mind? What was she doing in here? McCloud was crazy, absolutely crazy.

But there was no time to tell her that. No time to do anything but try to survive and bring everyone out safely.

It all depended on him.

"This way," he shouted.

Straining, he dragged his father's dead weight into an upright position. Bruce was as tall as he was and had about ten pounds on him. He was too heavy to carry. Slinging one of his father's arms over his shoulder and holding on to it tightly, Lance half dragged, half carried him toward the door.

Halfway there, he tried to turn around to make sure Melanie was still with him. The fire was growing fiercer with each second that passed. It obstructed his view. God, what if he lost her?

With the photograph frame tucked under her arm, Melanie struggled not to let Bess's weight throw her off balance. She kept her eyes glued to the back of Lance's head and concentrated on just putting one foot in front of the other.

"I'm right behind you," she called out. She didn't want Lance wasting any time by looking back. "Just keep going!"

The window they'd used to gain entry was completely framed in flames as the drapes on either side succumbed to the fire.

They couldn't get out that way. Debris from the ceiling was blocking the front door. The fire was swiftly eating its way to where they were standing.

Grasping his father more tightly, Lance kicked the burning debris out of the way. With effort, he grabbed at the doorknob. It was hot, just like the one on the other side, but he had no choice. They couldn't double back, and there was no other way out. He could feel his palm stinging as he yanked the door open.

Lance thought he heard Melanie scream above the noise of the fire just as they all poured over the threshold and down the verandah steps.

Letting Bess sink onto the grass, Melanie spun around and pushed Lance down. Startled at the sudden impact, he lost his hold on his father and fell to the ground. Melanie's cry rang in his ears.

"Your pant leg is on fire!"

He hadn't even realized that the flames had hooked their talons into him. Lance rolled furiously on the grass, acutely aware that Melanie was trying to beat the flames out with her hands.

Within a heartbeat, it was over. The flames were out.

Shaken, he sat up, looking down at the damage. The fire had only gotten one pant leg. The material was mostly eaten away, but it didn't appear as if the burns on his leg went beyond first-degree.

Right now he was far too numb to even feel them.

In the distance he heard the peal of a siren. They were coming. The guys from his fire station were responding. The fire wasn't going to spread to the other houses. It was going to be all right.

Relief strove to overtake him, but he couldn't let it come, not yet. Not until he was sure everyone was all right.

Scrambling to his feet, Lance checked on his aunt first. He took her hand in his. There was a pulse, and she was breathing. "Bess?"

Coming around, Bess coughed violently as she took in her first breaths of clean air.

"I'm all right." Weakly she waved Lance away, though she continued to hold on tightly to Melanie's hand. Then her eyes widened with fear as she tried to look around. "Your father—"

Mechanically, Melanie looked toward the other man on the lawn. Euphoric relief vanished, ushering in a new wave of fear. Bruce's chest wasn't moving.

"Lance, he's not breathing," she cried. "Your father's not breathing!"

The siren was getting louder. The fire truck was coming, and behind it, the ambulance. But Lance knew that even if the paramedics arrived in the next three minutes, it might be too late. Every second counted.

It might even be too late now.

He had to do something. Adrenaline stripped his exhaustion of its power. Galvanizing himself, Lance began CPR, praying that there was still time to save his father. And that he was good enough.

The first two efforts yielded no results. For all the pushing on his chest, all the breaths blown into his mouth, Bruce remained still.

Lance could hear Bess's panicky questions, but they just formed a buzzing noise in his head.

His father couldn't die this way, he just couldn't.

Lance tried again, pushing down harder on his father's chest before he breathed into his mouth. Mentally he counted out the numbers, then did everything again, more quickly this time.

"C'mon, Dad, c'mon." Lance stared at his father's face, watching for a reaction, willing one. Nothing. He fought off the bitter taste of panic. "You're not going to die on me now, damn it. You're not. I'm not going to let you. Do you hear me? I'm not going to let you die."

Barely able to think, Lance went through all the motions again, picking up the pace again. Tears gathered in his eyes.

A sudden barrage of coughing pushed him back from Bruce's mouth as Bruce belched out the smoke that had been choking him. He fell back weakly, but his eyes were open and he was at least partially alert.

"You always were infinitely stubborn," Bruce managed to say hoarsely.

Lance sat back on his heels, only vaguely aware that the corners of his eyes were wet. He was just too drained to move, too drained to even manage the smile that he felt through all the corners of his being.

"It's in the genes," he answered wearily, his voice hitching.

The next moment they were surrounded by a wall of noise as the firetruck pulled up and men in slick yellow gear jumped off, scrambling to bring the fire to its knees.

Paramedics swarmed around them. Lance recognized two of the three men. One helped him to his feet.

"I'm okay, see about my father and my aunt." He turned around to see Melanie moving back from Bess to give the paramedics room. "And my pain in the butt."

Melanie looked up sharply as she caught the description. Despite the number of people around them, she'd also heard the barely suppressed anger in his voice. She would have thought he'd be too exhausted to be angry. But then, exhaustion was a funny thing. It seemed to breed baser, more irrational feelings.

It certainly did in her. She felt angry herself, angrier than she could remember being in a long time. Maybe ever.

Moving out of the way of the activity, she glared at Lance. "You're welcome," she snapped.

She was bedraggled and covered with smudges from head to foot. Her eyes were flashing, and for once there wasn't even a friendly glimmer in them. He couldn't remember when he'd ever seen her looking more magnificent.

It also took everything he had not to strangle her. "What the hell did you think you were doing?"

Her eyes narrowed into dangerous slits as she raised

a dirty, pugnacious chin. "Hang gliding in the desert," she spat.

What the hell was wrong with her? Didn't she know what could have happened to her?

"Don't get flip with me," he shouted, ignoring everyone else around them. "You had no business climbing through that window after me."

No business? No business? her thoughts sputtered.

She was so angry, she had to concentrate hard in order to remain coherent.

"I saw your father's car parked across the street. I figured he had to be inside. You didn't know that, and by the time you came out with Bess, it would be too late to go back in. So I came in to tell you and to help if I could. You're not a superhero, either, you know." She rocked forward on her toes, drawing herself up. "And don't you shout at me and tell me what my business is. You have no idea what my business is, what I feel." God help her for even admitting this. "I saw you disappear into that burning building and my heart stopped." She should have her head examined for even caring. "In case you haven't noticed, I'm not the type to stay on the sidelines, wringing my hands and making little worried gasping sounds."

Without realizing it, she gave a perfect imitation of a hapless heroine in a thirties melodrama. Finished, she waved a blistered palm toward the house.

"You were in there, your aunt was in there and your father was in there. I damn well wasn't going to stand outside and wait to see if you lived or died."

She wasn't making any logical sense. "That was exactly what you were *supposed* to have done. I'm a trained firefighter. You're not. Damn it, McCloud, you could have been killed."

Her eyes were ablaze with challenge. "Well, I wasn't. Live with it."

Dumbstruck, Lance stared at her, speechless with anger, with relief, with more emotions than he knew what to do with. And then he exhaled a breath that he realized he'd been holding for a long, long time.

Leaning his forehead against hers, he said wearily. "I guess I'm going to have to."

Already the anger was draining away from her. "You could sound a little happier about it," she suggested.

He laughed softly, drawing away to look at her. "I am. More than you'll ever know."

"That's not right. You should make me know." A smile began to slip along her soot-marked mouth as her eyes searched his. Maybe they were in for a happy ending after all. "As a matter of fact, you should devote the rest of your life to making me know."

That was exactly what he intended on doing, he realized. Exactly what he wanted to do. But she could have at least let him take the lead for once. Still, he couldn't gather together sufficient pretend indignation to pull off asking, "Is it because you grew up on movie sets that you're always giving cues?"

Humor teased her mouth, though she tried to keep a straight face. "I wouldn't have to if you were just a little faster on the uptake."

Gingerly he took her into his arms. God, but she felt good. Even above the pain his body was only now becoming aware of. "I'll work on my uptake."

She smiled up at him. It hurt her lip, but that didn't matter. "You do that."

The ambulance driver came up behind them. "You two want to ride along in the ambulance?" Flannery looked from one to the other. "You both look as if the doctor should give you the once-over.'' He saw Lance's leg for the first time. "Hey, that's gotta sting like hell."

His arm around Melanie's shoulders, Lance looked at her and shook his head. "Naw, actually, she's rather painless once you get used to her."

"He's delirious," she told the driver. "Smoke inhalation you know."

The older man didn't bother trying to hide his amusement as he looked at Melanie. "Oh, I dunno about that." His eyes shifted to Lance. "Even bedraggled and sooty, she is one mighty-fine-looking woman, Reed." He sighed. "I should be so lucky."

"Well you're not." The remark even surprised Lance, though he was the one who said it. Covering, he asked Flannery, "How's my family?"

The smile was genuine and full of promise. "They're going to be fine."

Flannery gave Melanie a hand up into the back of the ambulance after the stretchers were loaded on. He waited for Lance to climb on, then slammed the door shut before hurrying around to the front.

Lance winced as he got in. His body was beginning to come out of shock. It wasn't happy about the condition it found itself in. But the discomfort was a small enough price to pay for what he had in return.

The space within the ambulance was limited, so they were all crammed together. Though he was facing Melanie, Lance found himself sitting up against his father's stretcher.

Bruce was alert enough to be able to take in the situation. "So, what do we do with the rest of the evening, son?" he asked weakly.

Lance turned to look at him. Until he'd been faced with his father's imminent death, he hadn't realized how strong his feelings for the man still were. How unwilling he was to let his father leave him behind permanently.

Bess and Melanie were right. It was time to end it.

"I don't know about you, Dad, but I'm too tired to do anything except be grateful that everything turned out all right."

"Yeah, me, too." He wrapped his fingers around the hand Lance silently offered him.

The truce was over, Melanie thought. Peace had broken out. Giving them a moment longer, she waited before leaning over toward Lance and cocking her head. "Say, do you hear that?"

Puzzled, he listened. But he didn't hear anything. "What?"

"That sound," she insisted, her head still cocked as if she was trying to figure out what it was.

Lance listened more intently, but there was still nothing out of the ordinary. "What sound? I don't hear anything."

"I do." A grin glimmered, then moved in. "It's the sound of hell freezing over." She looked at Lance pointedly.

He laughed then, recalling what he'd said to her about the day that he would make up with his father. "Yeah, I guess it is at that."

The laughter faded into something far more comforting, far more appealing. He looked at her, seeing beyond the dark streaks on her face, amazed at the woman who'd happened into his life through no action on his part. A woman who refused to leave no matter how hard he pushed her away or how much cause he gave her to go. A woman who would remain when he needed her.

"Want to skate on it together?" he asked quietly.

This time she cocked her head in earnest, trying to

understand what he was saying. Curtailing her impulse to leap to the wrong conclusion. She'd leaped enough for one night.

"Just what did you have in mind?"

He wanted to take both her hands in his, but refrained. "Marry me, Melanie."

She stared at him, saying nothing. Since she was never quiet, it made him uneasy. Finally, just as he was going to ask if she'd heard him, Melanie said, "Just how much of that smoke did you swallow?"

Was she going to turn him down? Or was she just as surprised as he was that he was capable of loving someone?

"Not enough to cloud my mind, if that's what you mean. Maybe just enough to clear it." Lowering his voice, he blocked everything out but her. "I need you, Melanie."

She'd done most of the work. That entitled her to make him twist in the wind a little now. "To fight fires with?"

He didn't take the bait. "No, to keep me from forgetting that there is a bright side to life. And that you're it."

The look in his eyes filled her heart. She'd reached him, she thought. Finally.

She still hadn't answered him. "I love you, Melanie, don't make me beg."

"No, I won't make you beg. But I will make you do something." She wanted to savor his proposal, to make it a memory she could press between the pages of time.

"What?"

He had absolutely no idea what to expect. It was going to be that way every day of their married life, he suspected. And he was looking forward to it. But she had to say yes first.

"Ask me again when I'm cleaned up." She looked down at herself. Her blouse was blackened and torn, and she'd probably never get the smell of smoke out of her jeans. Even her hair smelled of smoke. And she could just imagine what her face must look like. "I don't want to remember that I was proposed to looking like a Smoky the Bear ad for preventing forest fires. And I don't want you to remember it that way, either."

"You've watched too many movies," he told her affectionately. "This is exactly the way I want to remember it. I want to remember every single moment of tonight." His eyes grew serious. "Especially the way I felt when I thought you were in danger. Because that was when I realized just how much you mean to me."

If she threw her arms around him right now, she knew she'd embarrass him. Melanie struggled to curb the impulse. "Does that mean I'll have to start a fire every time you begin taking me for granted?"

"No." With his good hand, he cupped her cheek. "Just light one under me."

She wasn't going to cry, she told herself. She wasn't. Lance wouldn't understand happy tears. "I think I can manage that."

"Say yes, already." They turned to look at Bess. She was clutching the photograph Melanie had managed to save for her. The woman had absorbed every word as if it were life-sustaining medicine. "I'm going to need to buy a lot of furniture for my new place. I'd like it to be from your shop, Melanie, and it would be nice if I was entitled to a family discount."

"You got it, Bess," Melanie told her with feeling.

She turned to look at Lance again. "Right after we get back from the honeymoon."

Lance leaned in to kiss her. As soon as their lips touched, she winced involuntarily. Her lower lip was tender. She realized she must have bitten it while anxiously watching Lance perform CPR on his father.

He backed away, immediately apologetic. "Hey, I'm sorry. I didn't realize—"

Melanie slipped her good hand along his neck and drew him back to her.

"It's all right. I don't mind a little pain if it's for a worthy cause. Like I keep telling you, I'm stronger than I look."

Yes, she was, and he would be eternally grateful for that.

"C'mere," she whispered. "You're not getting off that easy."

"No," he laughed softly against her mouth, "I sure hope not."

*   *   *   *   *

Watch the sparks fly
between Melanie's mother and
Lance's father in
NEVER TOO LATE FOR LOVE,
coming only to Silhouette Romance
in February 1999.

Silhouette Romance
celebrates the joys
of first love in
VIRGIN BRIDES

September 1998:
THE GUARDIAN'S BRIDE
by Laurie Paige (#1318)
A young heiress, desperately in love with her
older, wealthy guardian, dreams of wedding the
tender tycoon. But he has plans to marry
her off to another....

October 1998:
THE NINE-MONTH BRIDE
by Judy Christenberry (#1324)
A widowed rancher who wants an heir and a prim librarian
who wants a baby decide to marry for convenience—but will
motherhood make this man and wife rethink their
temporary vows?

November 1998:
A BRIDE TO HONOR by Arlene James (#1330)
A pretty party planner falls for a charming, honor-bound
millionaire who's being roped into a loveless marriage. When
the wedding day arrives, will *she* be his blushing bride?

December 1998:
A KISS, A KID AND A MISTLETOE BRIDE (#1336)
When a scandalous single dad returns home at
Christmas, he encounters the golden girl he'd fallen
for one magical night a lifetime before.

Available at your favorite retail outlet.

Looking For More Romance?

Visit Romance.net

Silhouette
ROMANCE™

COMING NEXT MONTH